STAGE L

★ Lauren ★
Drastic Decisions

by Geena Dare

ORCHARD BOOKS

To Teagan

ORCHARD BOOKS
96 Leonard Street, London EC2A 4RH
Orchard Books Australia
14 Mars Road, Lane Cove, NSW 2066
ISBN 1 86039 645 3
First published in Great Britain in 1998
Paperback original

A CIP catalogue record for this book is available
from the British Library.
Printed in Great Britain

☆CHAPTER ONE☆

Crying in the Night

Lauren woke up to the sound of someone crying. At first, she thought she must be dreaming. There were no small children in her house, and it was the middle of the night. Lauren checked the square of darkness outside her window, then rolled over to look at the clock. 3:09 said the red letters. But someone was crying, downstairs!

Lauren climbed out of her warm bed, felt her way to the light switch on the wall, and found her dressing gown hanging on the cupboard door. She paused before stepping out into the hall.

The crying sounds were softer now – no longer wails, but sobs. Lauren tiptoed down the wide curved stairs of her house. A crack of light showed under the music room doors. The sobbing seemed to be coming from in there.

"Hello?" Lauren tapped on the sliding wooden doors.

There was a moment of breathless silence and Lauren tapped again. "Is someone in there?"

She slid open the doors. A baby grand piano stood in one corner of the room. In the dim light of the lamp over the piano's music rack, she could see her mother's bent head. Her dark hair hid her face.

"Mum?" Lauren tucked her own fair hair behind her ears and took a nervous step forward. She felt as if she was trespassing on a private moment. She had never seen her mother cry.

"I'm sorry I woke you." Her mother's voice was muffled. Her face was buried in a large photo album.

Lauren wished she had stayed in bed. "That's OK," she said. "What's wrong?"

Her mother swivelled round on the piano stool, clutching the album to her chest.

Lauren gave a gasp as she recognized it. It was her music scrapbook! Her mother had been going through all her old newspaper clippings. All those ancient pictures of her in frilly dresses winning prizes at music festivals!

"How can you ask what's wrong?" Her mother's face was in shadow, but her voice was full of blame. "Your singing teacher called today. She wants to stop your lessons."

Lauren felt a stab of guilt and anger. She'd been studying with Mrs Bainbridge since she was six years old. At her last lesson she had been furious with Lauren for not memorizing her practice piece. But how dare she call and say that to her mother!

"She says you're just wasting her time with this folk music you want to sing. Oh, Lauren! What's happened? You could do anything you wanted with a voice like yours – right to the top in opera, if you wanted – and you're wasting it on that pitiful performing arts school!"

"It's not pitiful!" Lauren felt her anger rise. Ever since she'd been accepted at the William S. Holly Stage School, she'd been having this battle with her parents.

"It's those friends of yours!" Her mother shook her head. "They're just not the kind of people you should be associating with! They're the ones who are turning you away from serious music."

"That's not true!" Lauren cried. She thought of her friends – the tall, beautiful Jenna, passionately devoted to dance, Abbi with her flying gold-blonde hair, and her burning desire to be a star, and Dan, with his funny, kind ways. And then there was Matt.

Matt Caruso's face had been in Lauren's mind from the moment she had met him at last summer's Stage School auditions. It didn't matter that he treated her like a little sister. It was really because of Matt that she was at William S. Holly, though she wouldn't admit that to anyone!

"I don't want to sing opera – why can't you understand?" Lauren pleaded. "Stage School is where my friends are, and where I want to be." But even as she said it, Lauren felt a pang. In the last few weeks, things hadn't been going well for her at William S. Holly.

But her mother's idea of an alternative was to go back to the very proper girls' school where she had been studying, and to spend every spare hour practising operatic arias!

She had no burning wish to perform, to sing opera in front of crowds of people. That's what her parents wanted – what they'd been training her for and pushing her towards since she was six.

"A talent like yours..." Lauren could hear the tears in her mother's voice again. "It's a gift. People dream of being able to sing like that, and you just want to throw it all away."

Lauren could hear footsteps on the stairs behind her. It must be her father, coming to see what was wrong.

"Let's go to bed, Mum," Lauren pleaded. She dreaded getting into this conversation with her dad, especially in the middle of the night!

"You go ahead," her mother sighed. Lauren slipped past her into the kitchen, and made her way to her room up the back stairs. She climbed into bed and clenched the covers under her chin, listening to the raised voices of her parents below.

"I just can't watch her throw her life away like this!" she heard her mother moan.

"Well, it does no good to stay up all night," her father was saying. "You'll just make yourself ill."

Lauren clenched the covers tighter. How much more of this could she stand? It was as if she'd left home and become a drug addict at thirteen, the way they talked about her!

☆

The next morning, Lauren's father was alone in the kitchen fixing a breakfast tray, when she went down. He turned to look at her.

"Your mother's not well," he said. "She didn't

sleep much last night."

"What's wrong?" Lauren asked, knowing what a stupid question it was. ***She*** was what was wrong, the cause of all the problems in their family.

"She's anxious about you," Lauren's father looked tired, too. "The news about your singing lessons came as a shock. She thought...we both thought you might get over this Stage School thing." He looked down.

Lauren felt her heart wrench. She and her dad had always been close. Now, he barely spoke to her, and when he did it was in this cold, flat voice.

"If you could just understand..." Lauren started.

"I know...your friends," her father sighed. "I'm afraid your friends are leading you down the wrong path – away from the music you love and your real future. I'm afraid I do understand."

He always cut off conversations that way, Lauren thought furiously, as she watched her father carry her mother's breakfast tray out of the room. Why couldn't she talk to him – tell him how she felt? She wanted to call after him, but the words just stuck in her throat.

☆CHAPTER TWO☆

Stage Fright

Lauren met Matt on the school steps that morning. As usual, her heart seemed to miss a beat. She took a deep breath so her feelings wouldn't show in her face.

"Lauren! Just the person I wanted to see!" Matt had brown hair that curled maddeningly around his ears, and an irresistible smile. He grabbed Lauren's hand and swung her up on the steps beside him.

"Come on," he pulled her up the rest of the stairs to the school's main doors. "We haven't got much time. It's five to nine."

"Time for what?" Lauren laughed breathlessly. Part of being breathless was the sheer speed they were moving, the other part was just having her hand in Matt's. "Where are we going?"

"The office," Matt grinned. "I want you to help me read the morning announcements. I'm the student in charge this week."

"Read announcements for the whole school? Oh, no. Matt, I couldn't!" Lauren pulled on his hand.

"Sure you could. It's easy. The secretary has it all written out. I introduce you as the most brilliant singer in the first-year class, and you just read the stuff into the microphone..."

"And everyone in the whole school hears," Lauren shuddered. "Matt, I can't. It's easy for you. You're cool...and everybody knows you."

"And you're shy, and quiet, and walk around the halls like a little mouse," Matt smiled into her eyes, still holding her hand. "It's time we raised your profile, Lauren. People should know how great you are."

They had reached the office door. The secretary was waiting with a typed list. "You're cutting it fine this morning," she glanced at Matt. "The bell's going to go any second."

"I had to wait for my announcer," Matt said. "This is Lauren Graham."

The secretary forgot her impatience. She couldn't resist Matt's good humour and smiling eyes. "Good morning, Lauren," she said, handing her the list of announcements. "Are you ready?"

"No!" Lauren protested, but Matt was dragging her towards the public address system. Her hands were clammy with nerves.

"I'll be right here if you get into trouble," he promised. "Just take deep breaths, while I introduce you."

Lauren concentrated on her breathing and tried not to listen as Matt told the most outrageous lies about her. Then, without any warning, he thrust the microphone in her face and said, "Over to you,

Lauren. What's going on at William S. Holly today?"

Lauren stared at the sheet in her hand, but her eyes refused to focus. "Uh…uh…" she stammered.

Matt peered at the paper. "Auditions for the one-act play festival this afternoon, right, Lauren?" he said, whirling his hand and nodding to show that she should talk.

"Uh…right," Lauren managed to croak.

"And then…" Matt coaxed.

"And…um…then…there are some talent scouts coming to audition actors for a TV commercial," Lauren managed to stumble on.

"That sounds exciting," Matt boomed into the microphone. "Do they just want actors?"

"N-no…" Lauren tried to read the paper, but it still swam in front of her eyes.

"Dancers, too?" Matt suggested, pointing to the words on the paper.

Lauren could feel the hot red colour in her cheeks. Her knees were knocking. She couldn't do this. Kids all over the school must be laughing at her, especially after that ridiculous build up Matt had given about her being the next singing sensation. She couldn't even talk into a microphone, let alone sing.

"Yes," she finally whispered in an agony of embarrassment. "They want dancers, too."

She thrust the sheet of announcements into Matt's hand, shook her head violently, turned and ran out of the office.

As she headed for the washroom down the hall, she could hear Matt's voice booming through the school corridors. "Thanks, Lauren, for giving us a hand today."

She could hear laughter coming from the classrooms as she ran past. They all thought it was a joke, another of Matt's gags.

"I'm a joke," Lauren thought, as she stared at her pale face in the washroom mirror. Her grey eyes stared back at her, wide with despair. How could she face her music class and Mr O'Brien, after that!

☆

Mr O'Brien's smug round face greeted her at the door. "Here's our Lauren," he said. "Had a spot of stage fright, did you? Don't worry. We'll knock that out of you in here."

Mr O'Brien was a bully, Lauren thought. He was always threatening to knock or strangle or destroy some bad habit of his students. Lauren felt her anger rise as she walked to her seat in the music studio. She kept her eyes straight ahead, even though she was sure the other kids were staring at her, or laughing behind their hands.

"Still, we should applaud Lauren for trying," Mr O'Brien clapped loudly. "Take every opportunity to sing or speak into a microphone that you can. It's good practice."

There was a half-hearted smattering of applause around the room. Lauren felt her cheeks go fiery red as she slipped into her seat. Why wouldn't he stop? She knew Mr O'Brien disliked her. She had refused to sing at the top of her voice, no matter how much he'd bullied and threatened her. That kind of screeching could destroy her vocal chords.

Her classical teacher, Mrs Bainbridge, would die if she ever sat in on one of Mr O'Brien's singing lessons!

Somehow, Lauren made it through the morning. By lunch time, she hoped kids would have forgotten the fool she'd made of herself. Not that many people know who I am, anyway, she thought as she braced herself to enter the big noisy canteen on the first floor.

The William S. Holly canteen was the nerve centre of the school. It was where everybody met to share news, see friends, do last-minute rehearsals and finish homework for classes.

Lauren slid some fruit salad and a muffin on to her tray and walked, head down, towards the table near the back that her group had staked out during the summer auditions. They had become a closely-knit group during those gruelling three weekends of try-outs, and now they always got together for lunch.

Lauren saw their table was deserted. She sat down with a sigh, hoping her friends would come soon.

All around her, kids were practising dance steps, humming music, practising lines. At the next table, one guy was juggling oranges and two other people were peering at publicity photographs. The noise was deafening.

Lauren kept her head down, and concentrated on her fruit salad. Then she heard a shout.

"LAUREN! I have the most amazing news!" Lauren's head came up gratefully. Abbi's shriek of joy rose above the babble. She came dashing up to the table with Dan behind her.

Dan is usually following Abbi like a loyal puppy, Lauren thought. He must feel the same way about her as I do about Matt.

"Dan and I did our scene this morning…" Abbi was so breathless she could hardly get the words out. She turned to look at Dan, her eyes glowing. "Dan was brilliant. He was so funny."

Dan gave a comic bow. Poor Dan, Lauren thought. His ears were brick red with Abbi's praise. He didn't have to try very hard to be funny. He had ears that stuck out, a long nose and a crooked grin that twisted up one side of his face. But he was really sweet and a good friend.

"And…" Abbi let out a long drawn-out breath, "Tony Martin, the guest director, said I had great talent. Great talent! Doesn't that sound wonderful?" Abbi was walking on air. "Dan and I are going to audition for the TV commercial tonight. Wouldn't that be wonderful? To be in a commercial that everybody sees?"

Lauren felt herself shudder. She couldn't imagine anything worse. What's wrong with me? she thought. Why am I so afraid to perform in front of people?

Just then she caught sight of Matt and Jenna, working their way through the crowd towards them. Jenna James really moved like a dancer, Lauren thought – so tall and proud. Her head was perched like a flower on the stem of her long neck, and her black braids were done up on top of her head, making her look even more regal. Her warm brown eyes were glowing at Matt, as they shared a laugh.

Matt shook his finger at Lauren. "Why did you run out like that?" he demanded.

"I've never talked into a microphone before," Lauren murmured. "I just froze."

"Don't worry," Jenna squeezed her hand. "People thought it was just Matt, fooling around as usual."

"Are you going to try out for the TV commercial after school?" Abbi asked eagerly. "Dan and I are."

"No," Jenna shook her head firmly. "We have to practise for our New York workshop, right, Matt?"

Matt made a face. "Work, work, work," he said. "Give up fame and riches for our art – that's us!"

But he didn't look unhappy, Lauren thought. He looked pleased and proud to be dancing with Jenna. They had just won a big dance competition, and the prize was a workshop class in New York.

"Did you find out when you go to New York?" Dan asked Jenna.

"During the spring break," Jenna spun round, hugging herself with joy. "Four more months...I can't wait."

Three weeks with Matt in New York, Lauren thought. No wonder Jenna looks so happy. It's her dream come true.

Suddenly Lauren felt like a fifth wheel. What was she doing here among all these sparkling personalities. They were all going places, doing things, performing, while she was too mousy even to speak into a microphone.

Maybe my parents are right, Lauren thought miserably. Maybe I don't belong at Stage School!

☆CHAPTER THREE☆

Pop, Fizz!

"Have you noticed how pale and tired Lauren looks these days?" Abbi asked. "Something must be bothering her." Abbi and Jenna were shoving books into their lockers after school.

Jenna looked down at her slim brown hands as she twirled the knob on her lock. "I don't think she's got over her crush on Matt," Jenna said. "She never talks about it, but I think it hurts her that Matt and I..." Her voice trailed off.

"You mean, that you two are going to New York together?" Abbi's bright blue eyes were alert as she studied Jenna's profile. "It's just a dance workshop. Do you think she's jealous?"

Jenna shook her head and shrugged. She was sorry she'd brought the subject up. There was more than just dancing between her and Matt, but the feelings were so new, and so important, that neither of them had put them into words. Matt, who never took anything seriously, hid his feelings behind jokes and laughter. While she, who was totally wrapped up in her dancing, pretended nothing had changed. But sometimes she caught

Matt looking at her with such a serious look! And sometimes, a bubble of happiness made Jenna skip in the air for no reason.

Even though nothing was said, both of them knew that something was different. Jenna suspected Lauren knew, too. Lauren was so sensitive and intelligent. She had stopped telling Jenna her secrets, stopped sharing the things that were bothering her.

"She's so quiet!" Abbi threw up her hands. "I can't break through this new shell. She's like a closed-up little clam."

Jenna let one corner of her mouth twitch up. Abbi overflowed with life and energy. It was hard to get past the sparks that flew from her in all directions.

"Oh, well," Abbi sighed gustily. "I guess we'll just have to watch and be there if Lauren needs us."

Jenna nodded. She decided to try to change the subject. "Are you and Dan ready for your big auditions for the TV commercial?" she asked.

The worried frown on Abbi's forehead relaxed a little, and her eyes lit up. "It's at four o'clock," she said, glancing up at the canteen clock. "I wish Dan would get here!"

"Your wish is my command," Dan said, coming up behind Abbi and leaning his chin on her shoulder. "What are you looking so serious about?"

"We're talking about Lauren," Abbi swirled around to face him. "Have you seen her?"

"I saw her leaving the school just now," Dan

said. "She looked like she had the weight of the world on her shoulders. What's wrong with her?"

"We don't know!" Abbi said. "She's been acting weird all week."

"I wish Matt hadn't pulled that stupid announcement gag on her this morning," said Dan. "Nobody likes to be embarrassed in front of the whole school."

"Let's try to talk to her tomorrow," Abbi suggested. "Maybe if we remind her how great she is and how we all love her...what do you think?"

"I think you'll just embarrass her more," Dan laughed. Abbi's way of dealing with a problem was to run smack into the middle of it, fists flying.

"Well, you think of something, then," Abbi said impatiently. "Come on, we should be going – the audition starts in five minutes."

"Break a leg," Jenna called after them.

"Thanks, we will," Abbi waved back.

☆

The TV crew had set up cameras in the school gymnasium. They had marked off a square on the floor under the basketball hoop where the actors were to perform. The gym was a tangle of wires and cables, tall light stands and cameras.

"Wow!" Abbi exclaimed. "This looks like the real thing."

Groups of students were standing around chatting, while the technicians set up.

"Quiet, everybody!" the artistic director called, appearing with a megaphone and gathering them around him. "Welcome to the Snappy Swig audition. We want a crowd of typical teens, drinking our product, and enjoying it, while they do typical teen activities – rollerblading, skateboarding, dancing, shooting hoops, blah-blah-blah. We are looking for lots of activity, no dead moments, fun, fun, FUN! Got that?"

There were nods and murmurs of agreement. Dan and Abbi glanced at each other.

"Excuse me, sir. We don't normally drink fizzy drinks while we're playing basketball," one senior student pointed out.

The artistic director put down his megaphone. "Well, for this commercial, you do. That's the whole idea. You drink Snappy while you're having fun. Got it?" He picked up the megaphone again, looking annoyed. "Anybody else want to make a comment?"

Nobody did.

"All right, then, we'll divide you into groups of ten. When it's your turn, we'll start the music, and I want you to give it all the energy you've got. There are blades, skateboards and basketballs over there." He pointed to a heap of props. "We'll shoot the actual commercial outside in real ball courts, rollerblade rinks, blah-blah-blah. Lots of different settings. This is just to see how you look."

Abbi and Dan dived for the pile of props. Abbi chose a pair of in-line skates that looked roughly her size. She plonked herself on the floor to put them on.

"You guys ready?" the director's assistant pointed at them. "You're in the first group."

"You unicycle?!" Abbi noticed Dan steadying himself against the wall on the one-wheeled contraption.

"Sure. There was a guy on our block with one of these when I was a kid. He let me ride it all the time," Dan said, circling round Abbi with expert control. "Ever rollerblade?"

"No," Abbi admitted, "but I've skated since I was six."

"On ice skates," Dan looked dubious. "Those are different."

"How different can they be?" Abbi asked, reaching for a second boot. "They just have wheels instead of blades."

She finished doing up the second blade and stood up unsteadily. "They feel great!" she cried, clutching the wall for support. "I'll bet I could whip around this gym in no time."

"I think the trick is stopping," Dan laughed, jumping off the unicycle.

"I heard someone say you just tip backwards on your heel, with your toe in the air," Abbi said, looking down at her feet. "I'm sure I'll soon get the hang of it."

The director's assistant was handing out opened bottles of the sponsor's product. Abbi took a sniff. "Ugh!" she said. "It's fizzy! I got bubbles up my nose!"

Her feet rolled dangerously in different directions and she clutched Dan's arm for support.

"Maybe you should skip the blades and just dance?" Dan suggested.

"They won't notice me if I just dance," Abbi shook her head. "I want to stand out. I've seen bladers swig bottled water as they swoop along the path. I'm sure I can do it."

"Quiet! – We'll have the first group now," the director roared. The music started, and Dan and Abbi pressed forward with the rest of the kids in their group.

"Here I go!" Abbi cried. She gave a great swooping stride with her left foot which sent her careering into a tall guy just releasing a one-handed basketball shot towards the hoop. Fizzy drink flew in all directions.

The force of the collision sent Abbi zooming off in another direction, still holding her bottle high. She bounced off a dancer, bumped into another basketball player, spilled more of her drink, and went into a spin.

Stop! Abbi told herself frantically. She tried to tip up one toe, but she was moving too fast. She flew forwards into the air and flattened two more dancers as she landed. The Snappy Swig in their bottles sprayed in arcs over their three fallen bodies. By now, thankfully, Abbi's drink bottle was empty.

"CUT!" shouted a very angry voice through his megaphone.

Abbi wiped the sticky drink out of her eyes and blinked.

"WHAT DO YOU THINK YOU'RE DOING?" howled the director. Like everyone else near the action, he was dripping with Snappy Swig. He stood over Abbi, the perfect picture of the enraged director, turning purple.

"I'm a little rusty on these things," Abbi apologized, looking down at the rollerblades. "I'm sure I'll do better next time."

"Get those blades off." The director's voice lowered to a menacing growl. "It will take an hour to clean up this mess. Do you know how much an hour of shooting time is worth?"

"Probably a lot," Abbi said, struggling to stand up. "But you don't have to be so nasty about it!" Her face was flaming red. "Just because I spilled some of your stupid drink!"

"SIT DOWN!" The director was bellowing again. "Take those blades off and get out of here. I never want to see your face on one of my sets again, do you hear me?"

He stalked away.

"I can't believe this," Abbi said, shaking her wet curls. "How can he be so mean? I was just trying to get some life into his dumb commercial. I hope I haven't ruined things for everybody. I hope he doesn't go to some other performing arts school because I messed up!"

"Oh, Abbi!" Dan was half-laughing and half-crying. "If you could have seen yourself – with fizzy drink flying in all directions. I can just see the commercial now," he posed for an imaginary camera. "When your fun's totally out of control – when you're just having too much fun to stop – drink Snappy Swig!"

☆CHAPTER FOUR☆

Showdown!

Lauren dragged her feet as she approached the big house where she had lived all her life. It was a chill November afternoon, but she was still in no hurry to go inside. There should be a sign over the door, Lauren thought: Home of Pure Classical Music – No Cheap Show Tunes or Folk Music Allowed!

Lauren opened the front door, slipped her bag off her shoulders, and went through into the kitchen. Good! No one was home. The message light on the phone was flashing. It could wait until she had had a drink and something to eat.

On her way out of the kitchen with a glass of chocolate milk and a sandwich, Lauren hit the playback button. It was her father's voice, tense and worried.

"Lauren, your mother's in St Margaret's Hospital. Stay there and wait for a message."

The milk tipped out of Lauren's hand and the glass smashed on the floor. Lauren stood, stunned, in the middle of the mess. The message tape was still playing. She heard pops and clicks, and a bright, cheery message from one of her mum's friends about a lunch next week.

Lauren's heart was hammering in her chest.

"Lauren?" It was her father's voice on the answering machine again. "Mum's all right. The doctor thinks it was some kind of anxiety attack. Anyway, she's going to stay here for observation for a couple of days. Stay there. I'll be home by five."

Lauren glanced at the kitchen clock. It was twenty-five to five. She took a deep breath, looked down at the spilled chocolate milk and started thinking in quick, jerky spurts. Have to clean this mess up. Broom – somewhere. Sticky – wash the floor. It was easier to think about cleaning up the broken glass and chocolate, than her mother lying in a hospital bed and it all being her fault.

Once the kitchen floor was clean, Lauren paced the living room, then went to sit down at the piano. It had always been a friend when she needed to pour out her feelings. She started to play a song, then noticed that the scrapbook of her singing triumphs was still on the music stand.

Lauren opened it. Her own face as an eight-year-old looked back at her. How hard her mother had tried to curl her hair! It was shiny, smooth and straight, and curls slipped out an hour after her mother had twisted and sprayed them in. And those stiff, scratchy dresses she used to wear to music festivals!

Her mother cared so much about all these newspaper clippings and photos. And now I'm ruining her dreams and all her plans, Lauren thought.

She flipped the pages of the album. It showed pictures of her winning first prize at one music festival after another. She must have won thirty of them between the ages of six and twelve.

That was the part I hated, Lauren thought. The festivals, the phony people and the dresses. Some of the music was OK – a melody floated through her mind and out through her fingers on to the piano keys.

Lauren thought of her father, teaching her to play, and of all the music that had filled the house; her brother Robert playing the piano, her mother the flute. There was always someone practising...

The front door opened. Lauren stopped playing, slammed the scrapbook shut and jumped up.

Her father stood in the doorway.

"How is she?" Lauren asked, her voice trembling.

Her father stared numbly at her. He looked rigid with worry. "The doctor thinks it's just nerves and overwork," he managed to say. Lauren's mother worked at an agency that looked after children with physical disabilities.

"I want to see her," Lauren said. "Can we go there now?"

Her father slumped into an armchair without taking off his coat. "I don't know if that's such a good idea," he muttered.

"Please, Dad, it's important. I promise I won't upset her. I just want to see her, that's all."

Her mother's room was quiet, and the light was dim, but the dinner-time hospital noises and smells surrounded them. Trays clanged and bells rang. How could her mother rest here? Lauren wondered.

"Hi, Lauren," her mother smiled. Her dad had warned her she would be sleepy, dosed-up on sedatives.

"Hi, Mum." Lauren squeezed her mother's hand.

"How was your day, dear?" her mother asked. She would ask how your day was if she was buried in an avalanche, Lauren thought.

She gulped. "I've decided to go back to Thorncrest," she said.

She could feel her father's hand on her shoulder.

"Are you sure?" Lauren could see the effort her mother was making to focus her eyes. "You want to go back to your old school?"

"Yes. No more Stage School. I kind of miss Thorncrest, and the kids..."

Her mother smiled a beautiful smile. "That's the best news I could ever get," she said.

"You should sleep now," Lauren's father bent down to brush back her mother's hair. "Lauren and I will be back in the morning to see how you are."

Lauren's mother shut her eyes, and they tiptoed out of the room.

"Dad, are you sure she's OK?" Lauren said, as they walked down the noisy corridor. "What happened to her?"

"She collapsed at work," her father said. "She's been doing too much lately."

"And worrying about me," said Lauren. "Well,

no more worries. I'm going back to Thorncrest."

"You shouldn't make any snap decisions, just because of your mother," her father said. But Lauren could hear the relief in his voice, even though he was giving her a chance to back out. "How about…your friends?" he hesitated.

Lauren thought of Abbi and Dan, Jenna and Matt. They wouldn't miss her. And she didn't really belong at Stage School. She had only gone to the auditions in the first place as a favour to a friend who was trying out. And then I met Matt, she thought, and it seemed like a good idea to go. But it wasn't. It wasn't ever a good idea, and now look what I've done!

Her eyes filled with tears. "I'm sure," she said. "I've been thinking about switching schools anyway. Don't worry, I won't change my mind."

☆CHAPTER FIVE☆

Lauren Makes an Announcement

"What happened at the audition yesterday?" Jenna asked. She was doing ballet stretches at the canteen table, bending one graceful arm over her head, and then another.

"Disaster," Abbi groaned, clutching at her gold-blonde curls.

"What? Tell us," Matt insisted. As usual, he was eating two large cinnamon buns before classes began.

"Abbi on rollerblades, that's what happened." Dan looked enviously at Matt's heaped plate. He never had the cash to buy food in the canteen.

"Think you'll get a call-back?" Matt asked. He saw Dan's longing look, broke off half a bun and handed it to him.

"Not in a billion years," Abbi said. "I soaked the director in Snappy Swig!"

Jenna laughed. She had a lovely, bubbling laugh that still surprised her friends. The new, happier Jenna was someone they were just getting to know. Since she had won the dance competition with Matt a weight seemed to have lifted from her shoulders.

"I'm glad you messed up the commercial," Jenna patted Abbi on the head. "They're always exploiting us, those advertising companies. According to them, teens just live for fun and shopping. They'd be surprised to know what we really think."

"But we could have used the cash," Dan groaned. "TV commercials pay serious money."

"And somebody might have discovered us," Abbi added. "Think of the great exposure you'd get in a national brand TV spot. Next time I get a chance like that – no more rollerblades!"

Just then she spied Lauren coming through the crowd. "Lauren!" she shouted, "I called you last night. Where were you?"

Lauren came slowly up to the table. There were dark circles under her eyes. She tucked her hair behind her ears and tilted up her chin. "I have something to tell you," Lauren said. "I'm leaving William S. Holly. Today. I came to say goodbye."

Her four friends gaped at her. Then they all started talking at once.

"Lauren, you can't!" Abbi sounded horrified.

"What's happened?" Jenna took her hand.

"It's my fault. I'm sorry about the announcements yesterday!" Matt apologized.

Dan's voice was the calmest. "Shut up, you three, and let her talk."

Lauren sat down at the table. "You know my parents have been against Stage School from the start," she began. "They really want me to be an opera singer."

They nodded. Lauren's struggles with her parents had started at auditions, and gone on all year.

"You've had an awful time," Matt draped his arm on Lauren's shoulder in his old brotherly way.

"My singing teacher dropped me," Lauren went on. "I had a big fight with my mother about it and then, yesterday, she...she collapsed at work. She's in St Margaret's Hospital, having tests."

"Oh, Lauren!" Sympathy filled Abbi's eyes. "How terrible for you."

"They say it's just stress," Lauren gulped. "But she has to rest...and not worry. I've decided I'm going back to my old singing teacher. And I told Mum I'd go back to my old school, too."

"But you can't leave Stage School!" cried Abbi. "You can't give up your dreams. And what about the Celtic music group? You promised you'd perform with them at Christmas."

"I don't know if I can." Lauren had been singing with a visiting group of folk musicians, and they'd invited her to perform with them during the school holidays. Lauren could feel the warmth of Matt's arm around her, and for a moment she felt her determination waver. Then she caught a look of pity and concern flash between Matt and Jenna.

"Is there anything we can do to help?" Jenna asked.

Lauren shrugged off Matt's arm and stood up. This was making things worse! She didn't need

Jenna's pity and she didn't want Matt as a brother. She would be better off not seeing him at all!

"No," she said firmly. "I've made up my mind. I've already checked with the office. They're arranging a transfer to Thorncrest. So…I'll be seeing you."

There was silence at the table as Lauren walked away.

"This is stupid!" Abbi raged. "What's the matter with us? We can't just let her go!"

Dan reached out and clutched Abbi's arm as she was about to dash after Lauren. "Hold on," he said. "Put yourself in Lauren's shoes. Her mum is sick, and Lauren thinks it's her fault."

Abbi collapsed back into her chair. "You're right," she sighed. "But what are we going to do? Can we talk to Lauren's father? You've met him, Jenna. What's he like?"

"Very highbrow," Jenna said. "The whole family's into classical music. They don't approve of the shows we put on at William S. Holly."

"So, we're not good enough for Lauren, is that it?" Dan said.

"Something like that," Jenna agreed.

"Well, I don't care," Abbi bristled, gathering up her bag and books in a flurry. "You guys can all just sit here, if you want to. I'm going to do something. I'm not going to let Lauren just leave like this!"

"Be careful," Dan groaned. "Remember the rollerblades."

☆CHAPTER SIX☆

Going Back

"Abbi, this is a really bad idea," Dan said, as he followed Abbi off the bus at a stop near Lauren's house.

Abbi was consulting a map Jenna had drawn for her. "Be quiet and help me figure out which way to go," she said.

"It's possible that Lauren really doesn't want to go to Stage School, you know," Dan went on, as Abbi set off down a side street. "Maybe her heart is broken, and she just wants to get away from Matt and Jenna."

Abbi whirled on him. "What do you know about it, Dan Reeve? Having a crush on somebody isn't enough to make you go changing schools!"

"Sometimes, Abbi, you ignore the obvious," Dan muttered.

Abbi stopped in front of a large white house on a corner.

"Abbi? What's the matter?" Dan asked. There was such a look of longing on her face that he was shocked.

"Lauren lives in a real house!" Abbi gulped. "It

reminds me of the house where we used to live – before Mum and Dad split and we had to move to the apartment." She reached for Dan's hand. "I've just remembered something – walking up to the front door, with my little brother."

She set off up the drive like someone in a dream. Dan followed, shaking his head. Abbi didn't mean to act like she was in some kind of play all the time – she was just naturally dramatic. But sometimes it was hard to take! Dan had an awful feeling about what was going to happen next.

Abbi had reached the front door. Solemnly, she seized the knocker and banged it, three times.

A tall man opened the door. He had Lauren's grey eyes, and a tired face that showed little expression.

"You're Lauren's father," Abbi said, in her most theatrical tones. "We're her friends, from Stage School."

Mr Graham looked like he wanted to shut the door.

"Just a minute, sir," Abbi said. "We've come to plead with you. Don't take Lauren out of William S. Holly. She belongs there – with us."

"I'm afraid I'm going to have to ask you to leave," Mr Graham said. "We're going to the hospital in a few minutes, to visit my wife."

"Come on, Abbi," Dan urged. "Let's go."

"You'll be ruining her whole life," Abbi went on. "She doesn't want to sing all that stuck-up old opera stuff – you should hear her sing folk songs!

Lauren's not a snob. She's one of us."

Lauren appeared behind her father. "Abbi, Dan! What are you doing here?"

"If these are your friends," Mr Graham said, "I'll leave you to deal with them. We'll be going soon." He strode away, leaving Lauren holding the door open.

"What did you say to him?" Lauren asked, looking from one to the other. "He looks so angry."

"I just told him you can't leave Stage School," Abbi cried. "That you're one of us."

"Really bad timing," Dan mumbled. "I tried to stop her."

"Oh, Abbi," Lauren shook her head. "You've made things worse than ever."

☆

The next morning, Lauren stood outside her old school, Thorncrest, shivering in the cold November wind, and trying to will herself to go through the double doors. All around her were girls in plaid skirts, green jackets and brown shoes. Lauren felt strange in her jeans and zipped jacket. She would have to be fitted for a new uniform – last year's uniform was too short and too tight.

A tall girl with a brown ponytail paused beside her. "It's Lauren Graham, isn't it?"

Of all people, Lauren sighed to herself, the first person I have to see would be Veronica Evans. Veronica had been in her class since Year One. She always found a way to make Lauren feel even smaller than she already did.

"Are you honouring us with a visit?" Veronica

said nastily. “Bringing us a great performance?”

“No.” Lauren shook her head. She started walking towards the front doors. All around them, heads were turning, as she and Veronica went up the steps.

Veronica tossed back her ponytail. “I thought you'd be much too busy at Stage School to come back here to visit us.”

Lauren moved toward the front doors. She was determined not to let Veronica stop her. Once I'm inside it will be OK, she told herself. Veronica might not even be in my class. But she knew in her heart she was already toast. Veronica would make sure everyone knew she had dropped out of Stage School.

“I have to go to the office,” Lauren murmured.

“Do you remember the way?” Veronica pointed down the busy hall. “See you later!” she sang out as she pounded away in the other direction.

Lauren made her way to the principal's office. Her feet felt as if they were weighed down with lead. She knew her father had already called to arrange the transfer. Now all she had to do was register.

“Miss Armstrong will see you in a few minutes,” the secretary told Lauren. “Have a seat.”

Lauren sat on the hard bench feeling like a condemned prisoner. Every girl who came into the office with attendance forms, or a late slip, stared at her.

Thorncrest was a total gossip factory, Lauren thought. They'd be buzzing about her in every class.

The minutes ticked by. A bell rang, and feet pounded down the hall. There was noise and laughter, doors banging, then silence again. First period was starting. The whole boring routine of Thorncrest came back to her. Sitting in rows in dusty classrooms. Trying to stay awake, as teachers droned on and on. Everyone in uniform, everyone knowing which girls were at the top of the heap, and who was at the bottom. Someone like Veronica thrived in that atmosphere. Lauren hated it.

Lauren tried to swallow the lump in her throat. The principal's door stayed shut. The secretary pecked away at her keyboard.

She's too busy to see me, Lauren told herself, looking at Miss Armstrong's closed door. I'll come back later. After lunch.

She slipped out of the office while the secretary was busy with a teacher, hurried down the hall and out of the front doors.

The cold autumn air felt like freedom. Lauren stood, dazzled for a moment, as all the crises of the last few days drained away. She would go somewhere, do something entirely different for a few hours.

The school was on a busy downtown street. As Lauren walked away from its familiar surroundings toward the centre of the city, she felt as though she was seeing it for the very first time.

☆CHAPTER SEVEN☆

Marco

Lauren sat on a park bench and rummaged in her bag for her wallet. She'd been walking for hours, and she was hungry. She found her wallet at the bottom of the bag and flipped it open. Good, she had enough cash for lunch and the bus trip home.

Suddenly, Lauren realized where she was. How had her wandering feet led her to this park? She sat back on the bench in amazement. One month ago she had been in this very same place, singing with the Celtic group at a folk music fair. The singers had visited the Stage School and Lauren had sung with them. They'd invited her to the fair, and Matt and Jenna, and Dan and Abbi had all come. She had sung right over there, under those trees. There had been leaves on the trees then, flaming in their autumn colours. Now the park looked bare and lifeless, the red and yellow and gold leaves fallen from the trees' branches.

The Celtic group's piper, William, had loved her singing. It was his suggestion that Lauren might do some performing with them at Christmas...Lauren remembered his twinkling blue eyes looking down at her from his great height.

Matt said he loved her voice, too…there, she was doing it again! Thinking about Matt! Lauren shoved her money into her pocket, her shoulders into the straps of her bag, and stood up. It was all over. The singing, the friends, the Celtic music connection. The adventure was over. She needed to get back to Thorncrest and register!

But first, she might as well eat before she faced her old school and Veronica again – she was feeling really hungry and cold.

As she set off across the park, Lauren recognized the main city bus station on the opposite corner. Large buses rumbled in and out of the bays along one side. After the music fair, they had all gone to a café inside the station for chocolate milkshakes and fries.

She could almost taste them as she crossed the busy street. The café was at the back of the bus station waiting room, and Lauren had to pass a row of homeless street people to reach it. Most of them didn't bother her – a few stuck out their hands half-heartedly, hoping for some money.

She didn't look left or right, but kept her head down as she walked through the bustle of travellers with their suitcases, bags, baby strollers and backpacks.

And then, suddenly, right in her path, was a skinny boy in a black T-shirt and torn jeans. He had greasy black hair falling into his face. The eyes behind the fringe of hair were dark and pleading.

Lauren stopped. He looked a few years older

than her, and taller. He didn't hold out his hand, but he spoke in a strongly-accented voice, struggling to make each word clear.

"Can you help, please? I'm Marco, I am refugee…from Bosnia. I am hungry."

It was the word hungry that kept Lauren from pushing past and ignoring the boy. She was hungry, too, but something about the boy's eyes told her the nagging pain in her stomach was a fiery agony in his.

Lauren didn't know what to do. She didn't have that much money and if she gave some to him, she'd have no bus fare home. But she couldn't go into the coffee shop and eat with him right outside the windows. It was impossible.

Lauren stood looking at the boy. He was carrying an old string bag over his shoulder, and he was wearing an ancient leather jacket.

"Excuse," he turned away. "I must to sit down."

She could see his legs crumbling underneath him, and instinctively she put out an arm to steady him. He leaned on her with a sudden, surprising weight. Unwashed, weary, and helpless, he clung to her for a second. Then he seemed to gather his pride. He straightened up, and stumbled over to the nearest wooden bench.

It was that brave gesture that decided Lauren. That and the bench, which suddenly reminded her of the bench outside the principal's office at Thorncrest, and the feeling of not belonging.

"Stay there," she said, holding up her hand as if giving a signal to a dog.

She wasn't sure he understood, so she kept an eye on him through the coffee shop window while she bought two candy bars and a large container of chocolate milk. Fries would take too long. Sure enough, he had given up, and was walking out of the bus station when she caught up with him.

She thrust a candy bar towards him. "Come with me," she said, and motioned with her free hand. "Over there." She pointed to the park across the street, a square of green in the city grey.

The look on Marco's face would have been funny, if it were not so pathetic. "I go with you?" he asked, not believing.

"We have to share the food," Lauren explained. "It's all I have."

Marco tore the paper off the candy bar and stuffed the whole thing in his mouth while they waited for the lights to change. She had to take his arm so he wouldn't get run over by a bus turning the corner. It made her feel strange to touch him – his arm felt like a stick inside his beaten-up old jacket.

Finally, they reached the safety of the park. Lauren gestured to Marco to sit down on one of the benches.

"Here," she said, opening the chocolate milk. She took a long drink through the straw and handed it to Marco.

He bowed his head briefly in a polite and gracious nod, and then slowly drank the rest of the milk.

Lauren munched her chocolate bar and

wondered what to do. Marco did not look well. He had eaten and drunk too fast.

"Thank you," he tried to smile. "I better now."

"You should rest a bit," Lauren said. "You still look green."

"Green?" Marco asked.

"You know, sick..." Lauren rubbed her stomach. "You ate too fast." She picked up the empty container and shook it.

"Oh, too fast!" Marco tried to smile. "Yes, but I so hungry. You save my life."

"What are you doing here?" Lauren pointed to the bus station. "How did you get here?"

"Too much big to explain," Marco shook his head. "I come with uncle to North America. He go home, no work. I stay with cousins. But apartment is too small, no one has job – I come to city. Need work," he shrugged.

"You're from Bosnia?" Lauren asked. She wasn't sure Marco was telling the truth. "Why did you leave?"

"Too much fighting," he shook his head.

"How old are you?" she asked him.

Marco counted out seventeen on his fingers. He tried to straighten his shoulders and look grown up. "Please, what is your name, angel girl, and how old you are?"

"I'm thirteen, and my name is Lauren," she said.

Marco stuck out his grimy hand. "Very please to make your acquaintance," he said solemnly, then his face twisted as a stomach cramp hit him.

"Lie down," Lauren said, taking his bag and

putting it like a pillow on the bench.

Marco hesitated. "Police say, move on, move on, when I lie down," he told her.

"They won't bother us. It's OK," Lauren promised. She sat down on the other end of the bench. Marco had started to shiver. He couldn't stay here. He was just...outside everything. She glanced at her watch. In a couple of hours she'd have to head for home. What was she going to do about school – and Marco?

☆CHAPTER EIGHT☆

Friendship

If things were normal, Lauren thought, I'd call home. Her mother was very kind-hearted. She would have figured out how to help Marco.

But her mother was in St Margaret's Hospital, and her father was beside himself with worry. How would she explain how she'd met Marco? The last thing they needed to hear was that she'd run away from school and was walking the streets! And the last thing they needed was Marco.

Lauren gave him the rest of her chocolate bar. "Save it for later," she told him, indicating his string bag.

"Thank you," Marco said. He put the chocolate bar in his bag and stood up. "I go now."

"But where?" Lauren asked. "Where will you go?"

Marco shrugged, and straightened his shoulders. "I must to find place to sleep, get bath. Then I get job."

"Come on," Lauren said. She pointed to the bus station. "Maybe they can help you there." She had seen a sign for travellers' information – maybe they would know a place where Marco could spend the night.

The small information booth in the bus station was surrounded by young people with backpacks. As Lauren and Marco waited for their turn, Lauren overheard scraps of information. There were cheap hostels for young travellers all over the city. The information booth had maps telling how to get to them. The problem was, Marco had no money at all.

Lauren stepped up to the young woman behind the counter, not sure what to say. If only Abbi were here, she thought. She could talk to anyone!

"My friend is a refugee from Bosnia," she blurted. "He hasn't got any money, and he needs food and a place to sleep. Is there anywhere like that?"

The girl looked from Lauren to Marco. "Why doesn't he ask himself?"

"He doesn't speak English very well," Lauren explained.

The girl looked suspicious. "There are a lot of illegal immigrants in the city right now," she said.

"Please, can you help," Lauren said. "I don't think he knows what to do next, and I…I have to get home."

The girl behind the desk still looked doubtfully at Marco, but she brought out a brochure. "There's the International Friendship Centre, on St George Street," she said. She opened the brochure and marked a route in black on a small map. "It's a short walk from here. They might help. Whether he's illegal or not, like you say, right now he needs some food and a warm place to sleep."

"Thanks," Lauren said. "Come on, Marco."

She would just have time to walk with him to the hostel, make sure he was all right and then catch her bus home. If she was a little late, she could always tell her dad she'd had to stay after school for something.

"Thank you." Marco was bowing and smiling at the girl behind the information counter. "You very good."

☆

The International Friendship Centre was in an old brick house near the university. Lauren knew she was near where her father worked, at the Conservatory of Music. It was dangerous territory. He often took an afternoon walk for exercise. What if she were to run into him now?

"Come on," she urged Marco, grabbing his arm and running up the steps of Friendship Centre. Inside it looked very drab. Though it must have been an elegant front hall at one time, now everything was painted the same dull brown; the radiators, the light switches, and the wooden stairs leading upwards. There was a bulletin board hanging on one wall plastered with handwritten messages for the foreign students.

Lauren stood uncertainly, wondering what to do. Was there a staff person somewhere, someone she could talk to about Marco? She could sense that he was wavering again, and when she glanced at him, his face was a horrible pasty white.

"Sit down," she motioned to the stairs. "I'll go and find someone."

Marco sank thankfully to the second step, and buried his untidy head in his hands.

Lauren peered into what was now an office, but once must have been a parlour or living room. She couldn't believe that she was being so brave, but she had to get help for Marco before she could get out of there.

There was a desk and an empty chair, filing cabinets, bookshelves, and a couple of tired-looking easy chairs. The whole room was painted the same sick brown colour as the hall.

"Can I help you?" A short woman in a bright green sweater came up behind her, making Lauren jump. "I'm Liz."

"Yes, I mean no." Lauren was embarrassed. "My name's Lauren. I met this boy, named Marco. He's sitting out there on the stairs…" she began, nodding in Marco's direction.

"I saw him," said Liz.

"I'm afraid he's not feeling well." Lauren explained.

"This isn't a hospital or a clinic," Liz said briskly. "We're an International Friendship Centre."

"Yes, I know." Lauren struggled to explain. Liz was about to throw him out. "But Marco is from Bosnia, and he needs help – friends."

"Another refugee," Liz sighed. "Let's take a look."

When she saw Marco, she shook her head sadly. She said a few words to him, in a language he seemed to understand, and he nodded his head. "Da, da," he whispered.

"He understands a little Russian," Liz explained to Lauren. "He can't stay here, I'm afraid. We have no facilities to help refugees. We work with students on foreign exchanges, that sort of thing."

"But where can he go?" Lauren asked desperately. "He needs food, and money."

"I know," Liz said impatiently, "I know. Look, the best I can do is send you over to the McCann Street Hostel. There's a woman there who is from his country…" She was busily scribbling on a piece of paper. "Here's the address, ask for Dragana."

Lauren took the small square of paper and looked anxiously at the clock. "How far is it?" she asked. She had no money for more bus fares and she was running out of time.

"McCann Street? It's about half an hour from here."

"Half-an-hour!" Lauren felt a rising panic. Marco couldn't walk that far, she was sure. "His shoes are worn out," she muttered. She had watched him limping the last ten minutes of their walk to the Friendship Centre.

Liz stuck her hands on her round hips, looked from Lauren to Marco, and sighed. "I shouldn't do this," she said, taking a key out of her pocket and walking back into the office. She unlocked a centre drawer and pulled out a metal box. Inside, the box was full of cash.

"Pay me back, when you're in the neighbourhood," Liz said. "I'll call you a cab." She handed Lauren some cash.

Lauren could have hugged her. "I will pay you back," she promised. "Thank you, Liz."

"Wait on the porch," she motioned. "The taxi will be here in five minutes."

Lauren didn't dare think about how late it was getting. The thought of worrying her father and mother was unbearable.

In a few minutes, the taxi pulled up. Lauren saw Marco shrink away from getting in the car. "It's OK," she told him. "You're going to a good place." She hoped it was true.

She gave the driver the piece of paper with the name and address of the hostel, and the money. "Take a small tip, and give him the change," she told the driver.

Marco looked frightened when he realized Lauren wasn't getting in the car. "Please, please come," he begged. His black eyes were wild with alarm. He grabbed her hand.

"I can't!" Lauren said. "I have to go home. When you get to the hostel, ask for Dragana. She can help you."

"Please, Lauren!" He sounded desperate.

"Listen, Marco, I'll come tomorrow. I have to go home now, but I'll come to see you tomorrow," Lauren promised. "Wait for me at the hostel."

Marco's face cleared. "OK, Lauren, I wait," he said.

What have I done? Lauren wondered as the cab sped away. This means I can't go to school tomorrow, either. I'll have to think of something!

☆

Jenna was tidying up her dance things – she put her soft black jazz shoes back in her bag, pulled on her warm sweat pants and sweater. Dance practice always cleared her head, made her feel peaceful and serene.

But today, the large sunny dance studio at the top of the school had not worked its usual magic.

Maybe she was missing Lauren. And feeling guilty. Jenna sighed, and studied herself in the mirror that covered one wall of the dance studio. Her tall, slender self stared back. She had almost got over hating being tall, and she liked her nose and her hair and her eyes.

But when she looked into those eyes, she saw a person she didn't much like. Someone who had stolen the guy her best friend was crazy about! She knew how Lauren felt about Matt. She had tried not to let her own feelings for him develop – even when their dance teacher had paired them up for the dance competition. Dancing with Matt every day Jenna had seen another side of him, and found out that, underneath all his careless teasing, he had liked her, Jenna, from their first day at Stage School.

"It's all such a mess!" Jenna told her reflection in the mirror. From the moment it was announced that she and Matt had won the dance competition and were going to New York together, Lauren had thrown up a wall to keep everyone out – especially Jenna.

She missed her friend. Quiet, funny Lauren was

the kind of person you knew you could count on. The kind of person you could talk to about your bad days and disappointments. And until now, Lauren had shared all her hopes and dreams with Jenna. How was she getting along? she wondered, as she bent down to pick up her bag. How had she managed with her first day back at Thorncrest?

☆CHAPTER NINE☆

Old Shoes

"How was it, being back at school?" Lauren's father asked, on the drive from the hospital that night.

"It was fine – the same as ever," Lauren murmured. Her dad made it sound as if she'd been on vacation since September and was finally back at a real school. "I have to get a new uniform, though."

"As soon as your mother gets home, she'll order it for you," her father nodded. Lauren noticed that the corners of his mouth drooped down as he stared at the road ahead.

"Why are they keeping Mum in the hospital so long?" Lauren asked. She was afraid of the answer, but she had to know.

"It's waiting for these everlasting tests!" her father said.

"But can't she come home and wait for the tests?"

"The doctor wants her under observation," sighed her father. "She's probably better off there, where everything is peaceful."

My fault, again, that things aren't peaceful at

home, Lauren thought. She wriggled uncomfortably, knowing she was glad her mother was safely away while she sorted out this thing with Marco, and got back to Thorncrest School. She wished she hadn't promised she'd go and see him in the morning, but the thought of his frightened, pleading face haunted her.

If only life wasn't so complicated. Why couldn't she be like Jenna, who only lived for dancing, or like Matt, or Dan, who thought everything was a joke? She found herself missing them all more than she could ever have imagined.

☆

Before bed that night, Lauren stole into her brother Robert's room, found a pair of his old running shoes and slipped them in her bag. At eight thirty the next morning, as soon as her father had left the house, she called the Thorncrest School number. She put a dish cloth over the mouthpiece, the way she'd seen in movies.

"This is Lauren Graham's Aunt Louise," she told the secretary who answered. "Lauren won't be coming to school right away. Her mother has been taken ill."

The secretary said how sorry she was that Lauren's mother was sick, and that they would hold Lauren's place open for her.

Lauren put down the phone, her palms sweating. It was the most complicated lie she had ever told.

Abbi would have called it a successful acting job, she thought. She would have got right into being Aunt Louise. Abbi would have loved the whole adventure of meeting Marco and trying to help him. It was just her kind of thing.

But it's not my kind of thing, Lauren sighed, and I hate lying. Maybe today she would find Marco safe and settled, with friends to take care of him. Then she could go back to her own, miserable mixed-up life.

Lauren stuffed her bag full of food, careful to take things from the back of the cupboard where they wouldn't be missed. Biscuits and crackers, some cheese spread and peanut butter.

Marco could live for a week on this, if he had to!

She had memorized the hostel address, and when she stepped off the bus on McCann Street, she found number 468 was right in front of her. Newspapers blew up against the fence, and a sad weedy patch of garden separated the shabby house from the street.

Lauren screwed up her courage. She marched up the front steps and knocked on the door. Inside, she could hear a baby crying, and a woman shouting. Was this the wrong place?

Then the door was flung open, and a large man burst out of the house, almost knocking Lauren off the front steps. He didn't apologize, just tore across the street dodging through the streams of traffic.

A woman came shouting after him, and shook her fist as he hopped on a bus going in the other direction.

She stopped shouting when she noticed Lauren

staring at her. Her eyes swept up and down Lauren's body and then zeroed in on her face. "Can I help you?" she asked. Her English had a thick accent. This must be Dragana, thought Lauren.

She tried to smile at the woman. "I'm looking for someone called M-Marco," she stammered. "I'm afraid I don't know his last name. He came here yesterday."

"What do you want him for?" The woman had dark eyes, like Marco's, but hers flashed with anger. Lauren wanted to turn and run, but she held her ground.

"I'm Marco's friend," she went on. "Is he here, please?'

"Yes, he's here. You come in and see, if you want." The woman held the door open for Lauren. "But don't bother him too long, eh? He's very busy." The woman brushed past her, into the house.

Lauren took a deep breath. She wasn't going to leave without seeing Marco and giving him the shoes. She opened the door and stepped into a small, square living room. To her surprise, it was crowded with kids of all ages, staring at a television, their frozen faces lit up by the flickering colours of a cartoon.

Lauren scanned them, but Marco wasn't there. Above the noise of the TV, she could hear sounds from a kitchen at the back of the house. Making her way along a narrow hall, filled with boxes, bundles and battered suitcases, Lauren came to a small, crowded kitchen.

Marco was up to his elbows in the kitchen sink. When he saw Lauren he stood still, then shyly dried his hands on the white apron he was wearing and took it off. A smile lit his pale face.

"Lauren," he said joyfully. "I thought you never coming back."

He looked so different that Lauren didn't think she'd recognize him on the street. He was wearing a green polyester shirt with two buttons missing, and grey cotton pants that were too short, but seemed clean. His long, fine hair was brushed back, and his face was scrubbed. Lauren took a deep breath. What a difference a bath made!

Suddenly she felt shy, the way she usually did around guys.

"I brought you some shoes," she said, holding up the bag."

Eagerly, Marco reached for the bag and took out Robert's old running shoes, looking at them with pleasure. "These very good shoes!"

"They're my brother's," Lauren explained. "I hope they fit."

Marco sat on a kitchen chair and put them on. Lauren noticed his feet were bare and she wished she had brought some socks.

"Very good," Marco stood up. "Thank you, angel Lauren." The shoes made him seem taller, made him look less helpless and odd, Lauren thought.

"Maybe we go for a walk…in the park?" Marco said, a happy grin spreading across his face as he loped around the kitchen.

"No walks today!" Dragana came into the kitchen through a back door. "Marco is working."

Who was this weird, bossy woman to give orders? wondered Lauren.

Dragana spoke harshly in another language and Marco nodded. He tied the apron back around his waist, went back to the sink and started washing dishes once more.

"He has no money," Dragana glared at Lauren. "He has to earn his way around here."

"Can you speak his language?" Lauren asked.

"Close enough," Dragana nodded.

"How did he get here?" Lauren asked. "Doesn't he have any family?"

Dragana shrugged. "He came with an uncle to visit his cousin at Beamsville. His family were all killed in the bombing in Bosnia. The uncle has gone back, but Marco stayed here. If he goes back, he will probably have to be in the army."

"So why didn't he stay with his cousin in Beamsville?" Lauren asked.

"The cousin lost his job. His wife is not working. They have three kids. They have no money." Dragana shrugged again. "Marco came to the city to try to get a job – but it is not so simple. Marco is illegal immigrant. He has to apply to for refugee status – get his papers."

"So…can't he apply?" Lauren asked. "Can't we help him do that?"

"Oh sure, we apply," Dragana shrugged again. "But he needs immigration lawyer, it takes time, and in the meantime, he has to eat. So he works for his food, he helps out around the hostel. He doesn't go for walks in the park."

Marco had his back to them. He was rattling dishes through the soapy water at a great rate. Lauren wanted to ask him a dozen questions. Did he have enough to eat? Did he have a room to sleep in? But she couldn't ask with this woman hovering around them. Dragana seemed to be some kind of a boss at the hostel. There was another young man peeling potatoes into a huge pot, and Dragana spoke to him now in a language Lauren couldn't understand. A third young man appeared with a bag from the supermarket, and Dragana questioned him sharply. He shook his head, looking alarmed.

Lauren looked across at Marco. He was glancing nervously at Dragana, too.

I'm not leaving until I'm sure Marco is all right, she told herself. She took a towel and started to dry the dishes Marco had stacked.

"What are you doing?" Dragana said harshly.

"I'm helping Marco," said Lauren. "That's OK, isn't it?"

"We don't permit volunteer work here," Dragana said firmly. "These boys work for their room and board."

"I brought some food," Lauren said, trying to think of a way to stay. She slowly unpacked the biscuits, the jam, peanut butter and cheese. "I was going to donate these, too."

Dragana looked sharply at her. "OK. You can help Marco," she agreed reluctantly.

Lauren could tell by the look in Marco's eyes, and the other two young men, that they were still hungry. She would bring more food, she thought to herself.

Lauren worked with Marco until all the dishes were done. At home they had a dishwasher and she had hardly ever dried dishes one at a time like this. But it wasn't a bad job, and when Dragana finally left the kitchen, Lauren had a chance to talk to Marco.

"How is it here?" she asked him quietly.

"Is OK, maybe." Marco glanced around the crowded kitchen.

"Are you going to look for a job?" Lauren asked him. There must be something he could do besides work at this hostel!

"Dragana say my English too bad," Marco shook his head. "No use to look."

"That's not true!" Lauren suspected Dragana liked having Marco in her power. "Your English is OK. And I can help you." She sat down at the kitchen table and pulled her notebook out of her bag. "Sit here," she patted the chair beside her. "I'll show you some stuff."

Marco pulled out a chair eagerly and sat down. Lauren started naming kitchen objects, and making Marco repeat them: toaster, stove, table.

"What kind of work did you do in Bosnia?" Lauren asked him suddenly.

"I was student," Marco said. "I study at university in Sarajevo."

Lauren stared at him in surprise. How could he

have ended up here if he was a university student? "What happened..." she hesitated, "...to your family?"

"The city was bombed," Marco told her. "We had no food or water. Then a water pump was set up in the street. We took our buckets to the pump. We knew the danger. There were snipers everywhere, many people shot. But we needed water. Then a plane flew over, a bomb fell, there was big explosion! My mother and father, and my sister...all died." Marco's eyes filled with tears.

Lauren wanted to hug him. She looked helplessly down at her notebook, then closed it. How could she be talking about toasters and tables when he had been through so much. "I'm...so sorry," she stammered.

Marco reached over and opened the notebook again.

"I need English," he said gently. "I must go on, start a new life here. That is what my parents and sister would want me to do. "Toaster..." he pointed to the toaster on the counter. "For bread," he said, and smiled bravely.

Lauren gulped. "That's good," she murmured, "you learn fast."

As they went on with their lesson, Marco moved around the kitchen, learning the names for all the household objects. In a few minutes, a whole gang of children had wandered in from the living room. At first, they watched Lauren and Marco with huge eyes. Then they joined in. Before she knew it, Lauren had a whole class of eager English students.

Some of them were eyeing the peanut butter and cheese hungrily. Lauren broke open the packages and jars, got a knife from the dish rack and began to hand out treats. She made the kids learn to say "Please" and "Thank you".

Dragana had returned and was watching from the kitchen doorway. Her eyes narrowed, but she said nothing.

The day seemed to fly by, and before Lauren realized it, it was three thirty and time to go. Her father might be checking in by phone to make sure she was home at four.

"I'll bring more food tomorrow," she said as she threw her notebook back in her bag.

"You come again?" Dragana asked.

Lauren tried to meet Dragana's steady gaze, but there was something about her eyes that made her shiver inside. Oh, if only Abbi were here to face her down, Lauren thought. Or Matt. He'd probably just laugh at Dragana. But here at the hostel, among all these helpless people, she seemed an overpowering force.

☆CHAPTER TEN☆

Abbi's Discovery

"Are you getting much homework from Thorncrest?" Lauren's father came into her room and stood looking over her shoulder at the open notebook.

Lauren had been gazing at the notes she'd made during the English lesson at the hostel, and thinking about Marco. She knew she shouldn't go back there, but Marco and the kids needed her. It seemed so much more important than school. So much more real!

Lauren blushed furiously, her mind racing. How could she explain to her dad about these notes? Where can I find a washroom? How much is this box of cereal?

"We're uh…studying current events," she gasped. "We're role playing, to see what it would be like to come here as a refugee, without speaking English, and with no money."

A smile lit her father's tired face and Lauren felt the guilt strike right through to her toes.

"What a good idea," he said. "Obviously, at Thorncrest they have you grappling with important issues, not just playing at performing."

Lauren thought she'd better get off the dangerous ground of school. "Why are there so many refugees here, Dad?" she asked him.

"I really don't know," her father sighed again. "I guess conditions in Eastern Europe are pretty miserable. You should see some of the kids hanging around the Friendship Centre, near my office. Some of them look like they haven't had a square meal in months."

Lauren gasped inwardly. She had totally forgotten about the money she owed the International Friendship Centre for the taxi ride. She bent over her books. "I guess I'd better get this done. I want to go and visit Mum later," she muttered.

"I think you should skip the hospital visit tonight." Her father patted her shoulder. "Your mother will understand that you have homework. She'll be so pleased that you're settling in at Thorncrest."

Lauren gave a sick nod. All this lying and making up stories was just getting her in deeper and deeper.

"There's one more thing," her father turned at the door. "That Abbi person called for you. I'd prefer you didn't call her back until your homework is done."

"Don't worry, Dad, I'm not going to call her," said Lauren.

☆

Abbi slammed her books down on the canteen

table. "Lauren's father makes me so mad! Lauren had to wait until she'd finished her homework before she was allowed to even talk to me!"

"You called her house?" Dan shook his head in disbelief. "You've sure got guts."

"Of course I called her house. Lauren's our friend, isn't she?" Abbi looked from one to the other. "Why shouldn't I call her, for goodness sake!"

Jenna nodded. "How did she sound?"

"She didn't call me back," Abbi shook her head. "That's not like Lauren at all..."

"She must be worried about her mum," said Jenna.

"Maybe it isn't any of our business," Matt suggested. "Maybe she really doesn't mind going back to Thorncrest."

"And giving up her friends, and her singing?" Abbi's eyes flashed. "Of course she minds! And it is our business. Remember how you guys all helped me when I was going off the deep end over Blair Michaels? When I wanted to be a star so badly I couldn't see straight?"

The other three looked at each other and grinned. The starstruck Abbi had been impossible!

"You didn't give up on me, and I'm not giving up on Lauren!" Abbi scooped up her books and turned to leave. "I'm going to go see her."

"How?" Dan asked. "Her father won't let you in the house."

"I've got a spare period after lunch. I'm going over to Thorncrest," Abbi said. "And if I can't see her, at least I can leave her a note and say I want to get together. It's better than nothing," she shot over her shoulder, as she strode away through the bustling canteen.

"There goes our Abbi," Dan said. "I hope she's not going to do more harm than good!"

☆

Lauren waited until her father had left for work, then she took some money out of the cash stash in her top drawer. Most of it was birthday money – hers to spend on what she wanted.

Next, she searched in the back of her cupboard where she found stacks of old picture books, and stuffed them in a canvas bag. The younger kids would love these!

Lauren hurried downstairs and raided the cupboards and the freezer for food. She piled frozen meat pies, cans of beans and some cheese into her bag.

She wanted to take as much as she could carry. She'd see Marco at the hostel one last time, she thought, pay back the money for the taxi to the Friendship Centre, and then it would be over. She would go back to school, be a good daughter, and not worry her parents...

But, at the McCann Street Hostel, she was greeted like a fairy godmother. The smaller children grabbed her hands, hugged her legs, and demanded to know what was in her bags.

"She is my angel Lauren," Marco protested with a smile. "You little ones cannot have her."

Lauren thought Marco's English sounded better

already. She handed him the bag of food to carry to the kitchen. Through the back door, Lauren could see Dragana and a short blonde boy of about nine. Dragana was standing with her hands on her hips, watching him unload his pockets on the back porch.

Chewing gum, candy, cigarettes – Lauren glanced at Marco in alarm. What was a nine-year-old doing with cigarettes? The whole hostel smelled of stale smoke! But surely no one would sell cigarettes to such a young child?

"Who are the cigarettes for?" she asked Marco.

He shook his head. "Dragana teaches them to take things from the store without pay. She wants to teach me, but I don't want."

Lauren felt fear shoot through her. "Oh, no! Marco you mustn't! The police will catch you – shoplifting would just give them a perfect excuse to throw you out of the country."

"Dragana says we must work for her..." Marco was still watching Dragana and the boy through the open door, " ...since we can get no other jobs."

"That's not true. I'm sure you can get a job!" Lauren said desperately. "Marco, you don't have to do what Dragana says."

Marco's eyes were wary and tired, but he tried to smile. "Don't worry, Lauren. You come every day, and pretty soon I speak English like a professor. Then I get job."

Lauren felt her desperation choke her. "You need to go to a real school," she said. "You need to get out of here and find a safer place to live. The government will help…"

"No!" Marco shot up his hand. "No government. I have not papers. Dragana says they deport me back to Bosnia. There I have to fight in army again. Maybe I die."

Lauren stared at him. He was only four years older than she was, but already he had been a soldier. It was impossible to imagine skinny, pale Marco, with his gentle smile and his hair falling in his eyes, carrying a gun!

Lauren felt helpless fury as she watched Dragana scoop up the items the small boy had stolen. If it weren't for Marco, she'd report that woman to the police! She couldn't just walk away and leave him there. It wasn't safe.

☆

Abbi marched into the main office at Thorncrest and dumped her old purple bag on the counter. "I'm looking for Lauren Graham," she announced.

"Lauren Graham?" The pearls around the secretary's neck seemed to tighten with disapproval at this wild, untidy girl in jeans. "I'm afraid Miss Graham is not a student here, at the moment."

Abbi stared at her. "She's not?"

"No, she's not." The secretary looked down her nose at Abbi's battered purple bag. "Now, if you don't mind, we're very busy."

"But she was supposed to register this week!" Abbi persisted.

"I believe there was some family problem," the secretary murmured.

"Yes, I know, but…" Abbi let her voice trail off. She could be getting Lauren into trouble, she realized, if she said too much. She slid her bag off the counter and left the office.

The halls were a sea of green blazers and plaid skirts. Abbi stopped one of the girls who looked about her own age. "Excuse me, do you know Lauren Graham?"

Quickly, a circle of curious faces gathered around her.

"My name's Veronica Evans. I'm a friend of Lauren's." A tall girl with a challenging look stepped forward. "Lauren was supposed to come back here, but she only showed up for one day."

"Do you know what happened to her?"

"When is she coming back?"

"Do you go to that Stage School?"

The questions flew at Abbi from all directions. She tossed back her gold-blonde curls and stared at the circle of faces. "I'm Lauren's friend from William S. Holly," she said. "If you see her, tell her Abbi was looking for her."

☆CHAPTER ELEVEN☆

Squeegee Kids

Lauren made a decision. "Marco, come with me," she said. "I have to take this cash back to the Friendship Centre – remember?" She took the money out of her wallet to show him.

"Near the beautiful park," Marco nodded. "That was best day of my life."

"The lady we talked to, Liz, seemed nice. She might know where you can get help," Lauren said. "It's not the government, don't worry. They help students."

"I cannot go," Marco said. "I must today be squeegee kid."

Lauren's grey eyes widened in alarm. "You're going to be one of those kids who stands at the corner and cleans peoples' car windows when they stop for a red light?" she asked. "My father hates those kids."

Marco nodded in the direction of Dragana. "She says I must go."

Lauren tried to picture Marco in traffic, learning the complicated ballet of getting a driver's permission to wash the window with a squeegee while the light was red, getting paid and back safely to the curb before the traffic swept over him.

She shook her head. There was too much he didn't know about how things worked here. "You'll never survive out there alone," she told Marco. "I'll have to go with you."

Just then, Dragana came into the kitchen. Her eyes swept over the gifts of food and books that Lauren had brought, and the money in her hand. "You're a nice girl," she said, "but you shouldn't hang around here. Bring the stuff, then go." She waved her hand towards the door.

Marco followed Lauren to the dim front hall. "I am sorry, Lauren," he said mournfully. "I like to go to Friendship place with you, but cannot."

"It's OK. I'll wait for you at the corner," Lauren told him. "When you go out to do the squeegee job, I'll go with you."

Maybe, later, she could get him to the Friendship Centre, she thought to herself.

☆

"I can see why Lauren can't stand that stuffy school," Abbi whispered to Dan as they did their warm-up exercises in the drama studio. "I could tell the girls had all been talking about her behind her back."

Abbi threw herself back on the mat. "But the question is...where has she been since Monday, if she hasn't been at Thorncrest?"

"Maybe she just stayed home?" Dan suggested. "It's only been three days."

"Quiet!" Miss Madden, the drama coach,

warned. "I want total concentration. Relax! Picture yourself in a beautiful place – a place you love to be..." Miss Madden was a towering figure in a blue tunic. She was a good teacher, and Abbi usually loved her relaxation exercises.

But today, her mind was on Lauren. Abbi lay flat, her hair spread around her face, not thinking of a beautiful place, but of where Lauren might be. The thought was not relaxing!

"We can't ask her father," she said, sitting bolt upright after the exercise. "He thinks she's at school."

"You're really worried about her, aren't you?" Dan said.

"She's the sort of person you do worry about," Abbi nodded. "She's so small, and quiet, but you can tell she's more sensitive than the rest of us. Wherever she is, I'm sure she's not having a good time right now."

☆

The three lanes of traffic swept towards the busy, downtown corner. The cars paused at the red light like a flock of birds perching on a branch.

Six kids, carrying buckets of water and plastic squeegees like the ones at gas stations, darted into the road, up to the cars. They pointed to the windows and, if the driver waved them away, raced on to the next car. If the driver nodded yes, they dipped and rubbed and squeegeed the window clean, then raced back to the curb as the light turned green.

Lauren and Marco worked side by side. Lauren

was breathless with the risks they took. It was a thrill when someone nodded yes, and they raced against the red light to finish in time. Sometimes, before they got paid, they were pressed against the car as the traffic surged ahead.

Marco was pretty hopeless. Every time Lauren glanced across at him, his hair was in his eyes and he couldn't tell if drivers were saying yes or no. People blasted him with their horns if he got it wrong, as he washed their windows by mistake.

People either hated and feared the squeegee kids, like Lauren's parents, or thought they were brave and enterprising to find work for themselves.

"I cannot to do this," Marco panted, as they waited for a red light at the corner. "I make no money!" He looked dazed and grey around the mouth. He was shivering in the cold wind.

But Lauren's pockets were getting full. She was good at picking up the drivers' signals, fast with the squeegee, and light on her feet. The constant running and dodging was keeping her warm.

"It's OK," she told Marco. "I'll give you what I make. Here, go and get us a hot drink." She handed Marco some change and pointed to a coffee shop on the corner.

The light changed, and Lauren dived back into the traffic. Never, in all her carefully brought up life, had she been on the streets like this – felt the pavement, the hot breath of car exhaust, and the hurry and rush of the city. It was dangerous, but exhilarating. Nothing in her life, up to now, had ever felt like this.

☆

"OK," Abbi said to the circle of faces at the table in the canteen. "I went to the school and she wasn't there. She's never even been there, according to the other kids. So what are we going to do?"

Jenna put her slender brown arms above her head and did a stretch. She brought them down, gracefully crossed, in front of her waist. "Shouldn't we tell Lauren's father?" she suggested.

Matt nodded in agreement. "If Mr Graham knows that Lauren isn't going back to Thorncrest – for whatever reason – maybe he'll let her come back to Holly. I mean, any school is better than dropping out."

"But that would be betraying Lauren," Abbi agonized. "What if there's a good reason she isn't at school?"

"Such as?" asked Jenna. "It seems to me she must be in some kind of trouble. We can't just keep quiet, out of loyalty, when she may be in danger."

"What do you think?" Abbi turned to Dan. He had been very quiet through this conversation.

"I think," Dan looked into Abbi's bright blue eyes and spoke firmly. "I think we're Lauren's friends, and she trusts us. She's unhappy, her mother is sick, and she can't tell her father the truth. If we tell on her, she'll have no one."

"So, it's a stalemate," Matt said. "Two for telling Lauren's dad, two against. I say we wait one or two more days, keep trying to call Lauren at home at night, and then, if we still don't get in touch, and she's still not at Thorncrest, we have to tell somebody."

"Fair enough," Abbi nodded, and the rest agreed.

"I'll call Lauren tonight," Matt suggested. "Mr Graham doesn't know me."

Jenna glanced at Matt from under her long, dark lashes. He didn't know what he was doing, she sighed inwardly. Matt always treated Lauren like a little sister. He didn't know how much he was part of her misery. Maybe it wasn't such a good idea if he called.

☆CHAPTER TWELVE☆

Matt Calls

Lauren made a lot of money, all in coins. It would take too long to count. Flushed and excited, she handed it all to Marco. He had spent most of the last hour safely on the curb, or running back and forth to the garage for clean water.

Lauren glanced at her watch. Three thirty already! There was no time now to take Marco to the Friendship Centre. She would just have time to get there herself, on her way home.

"Don't give all the money to Dragana," Lauren warned, as she watched Marco stuff the money in his pockets.

"You coming back to hostel?" Marco looked worried and exhausted.

"No," Lauren shook her head. "I have to go and pay back the Friendship Centre, and then go home." She took a deep breath. Marco looked so crushed. He was older than she was, but right now, Lauren thought, he looked like a helpless little kid. "I'll see you at the hostel tomorrow," she promised. She couldn't just leave Marco at Dragana's mercy, or think of him out here on the street, alone.

"Hey, see you, Lauren," the other squeegee kids waved and called as they left. She knew she had earned a certain respect for her day's work from this band of street warriors. For some reason it made her feel crazily proud.

At the Friendship Centre, she waited impatiently for Liz. If she didn't leave soon, she wouldn't be home before her dad. And there was always the risk of running into him on the street in this neighbourhood!

At last Liz appeared. "I'm sorry it took so long to pay you back for the taxi," Lauren said, handing her the fistful of money.

"Thanks," the woman smiled, as she unlocked the drawer and put the money in the cash box. "I didn't really expect to see you again. How's your friend?"

"Not good," Lauren shook her head. "I wanted to talk to you about that. I have to find a better place for him to stay."

"He should really see an immigration lawyer," the woman advised. "If he's a refugee..." She looked at Lauren closely. "Have you asked your parents to help?"

Lauren moved quickly to the door. "How much would a lawyer cost?"

"More than you could afford," the woman shrugged. "You really should get your parents involved."

"I'll ask them," Lauren said. She was thinking of the squeegee job. If she could make so much money on her first day, she might be able to make enought to pay for a lawyer.

☆

Matt called Lauren from his own room in the basement, away from the big ears of his little brother and sister.

"Mr Graham?" he asked when Lauren's father answered the phone, "this is Matt Caruso, Lauren's friend. May I speak to her?" He tried to use the voice he used to speak to customers in his family's fruit and vegetable shop – polite, but businesslike. No apologies.

"I'll see if Lauren can come to the phone," her father said abruptly. Matt shook his head. Wow! This guy sounded tough.

It was Lauren's voice he heard next. "Hi, Matt. How are you?"

"I'm great," Matt swallowed. "How...are you?"

"Fine."

"How's school?"

"Fine, I guess."

This conversation was not going the way Matt had expected. "We all miss you at Stage School," he said.

"Well, that's nice. Listen, I have to help my dad do the…dishes. I have to be going." Lauren's voice was giving nothing away. Matt suddenly realized her father was probably listening.

"OK, Lauren," he said. "Nice talking to you."

"Thanks, Matt. 'Bye."

Lauren put down the phone, her hands sweating. Why did it have to be Matt who called?

Maybe Abbi and Jenna had put him up to it, she thought angrily. They knew she went limp as a wet noodle when she heard Matt's voice. Well, not any more! She had more important things on her mind, like fighting for Marco.

She heard her father's footsteps on the stairs.

"Everything all right?" he asked from her bedroom doorway.

"Fine," Lauren nodded. "I have a lot of homework."

"I won't keep you from it," her father turned to go. "But I wanted to talk about your mother, for just a moment."

Lauren sat up straight, and braced herself for bad news. They had visited her mother briefly after dinner. She still seemed so unlike herself, that Lauren had been startled. She didn't seem to be getting better in the hospital.

"The doctor doesn't think there's anything physically wrong," her father sat on the bed with his head in his hands. "They think she may be suffering from depression."

"What does that mean," Lauren said. She felt another stab of guilt – her mum had been acting depressed ever since she went to Stage School.

"Well, for one thing, it means she'll be in St Margaret's for a while longer," her father said. "They're trying to find the right dose of medication for her."

"Is she going to be all right?" Lauren gulped.

"Yes," her father looked up. "But the psychiatrist who's looking after her is worried about you, too.

He would like you to come in for a chat. He says it's normal for teens to feel guilty when something like this happens to their parents."

"Oh, I see." Lauren let her hair slide down on both sides of her face to cover her feelings. The last thing she wanted to do was chat to some psychiatrist!

"We can talk about it later..." Her father stood up. "I just wanted to let you know. I knew you were worried. Get back to your homework now."

"OK, Dad," said Lauren. "If anyone else calls – will you say I'm not home?"

☆

"Well?" Abbi grabbed Matt on the way to the dance studio the next morning, "How did it go?"

"Weird," Matt said. He shifted his dance bag to his other shoulder and gazed at Abbi. "It was like talking to someone I didn't even know. Maybe her dad was listening, maybe she just didn't want to talk to me, I couldn't tell. So we still don't know what's going on, or where she goes when she isn't at school."

"What will we do now?" Abbi asked. "I feel like Lauren is drifting away from us."

Just then, Dan came down the hall. He was carrying a video cassette case and wearing a broad grin. "Guess what?" he said. "Someone in the third year acting class filmed our fizzy drink audition last week. It's all on this tape."

Abbi looked horrified. "You mean all that slipping and sliding and making an idiot of myself on rollerblades is on video?" she screeched. "Give me that! I'm going to destroy it."

"No you're not!" Dan held it out of Abbi's reach. "This is a classic. I've got some ideas for things to do with it..."

"You wouldn't! Dan!"

"I'm just teasing," he laughed. "So, how did your phone call to Lauren go?" He turned to Matt.

"She was so funny and distant, I wasn't sure I was even talking to Lauren," Matt said. "She hung up as soon as she could get rid of me."

"I'd give my right arm to know what she's up to," Abbi said. "Where does she go all day?"

☆CHAPTER THIRTEEN☆

Dragana

Lauren sprang out of bed at the first buzz of her alarm. Her clock said just seven. Lauren thought about her mother, waking up in the hospital, and she swallowed a lump of guilt. Mum would get better! She had to!

She looked out of her window. The streets were still dark and the sounds of the city were only just beginning. Next week, Lauren thought, I'll go to school, and get good marks. Just one more day – that's all I need to get Marco sorted out.

Lauren dressed in suitable clothes for washing car windows in the street – an old jacket with a frayed collar, worn and patched jeans and work boots, and a bandanna around her fair hair to keep it from falling in her eyes. She glanced at herself in the mirror. What would Matt and her other Stage School friends think if they could see me like this, she wondered. I'll bet they'd be surprised!

By 8.30 she and Marco were on the street corner, washing windows in the rush hour. It was a miserable rainy morning and the cars splattered them with dirt. Lauren was pleased to see she looked just like the other squeegee kids, but maybe a bit smaller and younger than the rest of them.

She washed the car windows like a demon, feeling the weight of money in her jeans pocket getting steadily heavier.

If a driver shook his head to say no, she'd give him a cheerful wave and dash off to the next car. She left drivers smiling, waving back.

Marco's squeegee skills improved by watching her. He would toss the hair out of his eyes with a flourish, lean into the window cleaning with a wide grin, and thrust out his hand for payment with a bow.

He was actually starting to make money!

By noon, Lauren figured, they might have enough money between them to go to a lawyer. Every car cleaned brought help closer for Marco.

At ten o'clock, Lauren looked up to see Dragana, watching them from the curb. She was wearing a belted rain coat, with a hood covering her dark hair.

"You're having a good day, eh?" she said, as they crossed to the curb on a red light. "You make lots of money?"

Lauren flashed a warning look at Marco. "Not too bad," she muttered. She might have known Dragana would show up to check on him.

"Lauren, I watch you. You're very good." Dragana towered over her. "But you're soaked from the cars and the rain. Come on, take a break. I have a friend who has a café round the corner.

Let me buy you coffee."

Lauren hesitated. She was suddenly ravenous, just thinking about food. And Marco looked, as usual, as if he were ready to faint from hunger.

"OK," Lauren panted. "Half an hour break, what do you say, Marco?" She threw her squeegee into the bucket.

Marco nodded. "What do you say when something is very good idea?" he asked.

"Oh, you know, fantastic, great, cool," Lauren said. She smiled at Marco. He was really trying to pick up English and he was a fast learner.

Dragana led them to a café so narrow there was only room for the counter at the front and a single row of tables along one wall. She motioned them to a small one near the back.

"What you want? Coffee? Cake? What?" She took off her coat and slung it over the back of the chair. Under it she had on her dusty black sweater and skirt.

"Hot chocolate, if they have it," Lauren said. She needed something sweet and filling. She and Marco slid their buckets under the table. It felt good to sit down.

"For me, too," Marco nodded. "And a bun would be very fantastic."

Dragana went in the back. They heard her exchange greetings with the cook, and a few minutes later she came back with a tray loaded with hot drinks and sweet sticky buns.

"So," she said, unloading the food in front of the famished Marco. "You are good squeegee kids, you two."

Marco could only nod. His mouth was already full. He pointed at Lauren. "She…good," he mumbled.

"You happy working with Marco, eh?" Dragana said. "You like it down here – nice friends, nice work?"

Lauren just nodded. She couldn't very well tell Dragana what she thought of her while she was drinking her hot chocolate.

"You have trouble at home?" Dragana's eyes burned into hers. "Maybe you fight with your parents all the time? You think about running away?"

It scared Lauren to see how easily Dragana saw into her. What was she leading up to?

"No, my parents are – fine," she said.

"You're pretty young to be on the street," Dragana shrugged. "No school, no job, just hanging around the hostel."

Lauren stood up. "Don't worry, I won't be hanging around much longer. And speaking of jobs, Marco and I should get back to our squeegees." She drained her cup of hot chocolate in one gulp and stood up. Marco, looking disappointed, stuffed the rest of his bun in his mouth and loyally joined her.

"I coming…" he nodded.

"What's your hurry?" Dragana shrugged. "Sit down…finish…it's cold out there."

"No. We have to go…" said Lauren.

She stopped, clutching the edge of the table.

Suddenly, her head was whirling, the round table was spinning. What on earth was happening to her?

"You don't feel so well?" Dragana's big face swam before her eyes. "Too much work – you tired. Come back to the hostel and lie down."

Lauren didn't want to go back to the hostel. She wanted to make more money, and get Marco a lawyer. But her head ached so much she could hardly see.

"Here, Marco," Dragana ordered sharply. "Help me. We take her back to the house."

☆

"We've got a second chance!" Dan was jumping up and down with excitement. "They're auditioning another TV commercial after school." They were in the drama studio, waiting for Miss Madden's class to begin.

"The same director?" Abbi asked, doubtfully. He had seemed very sure he never wanted to see Abbi again.

"No, this is a different company. This is for acne cream. Matt and Jenna are going to try out. Are you up for it?"

"But I don't have…" Abbi rubbed her hand over her smooth face, " ...at least, not right now."

"That's what make-up is for," Dan laughed. "They'll make you look all spotty for the camera. If you really had zits, they couldn't take them away with the magical miraculous cure, could they? Well? Are you going to try out?"

"Are you?" Abbi asked.

"Of course. I keep dreaming of that big TV money, you know me," said Dan.

Abbi gave his arm a squeeze. Underneath Dan's light-hearted teasing, she knew he was really serious about needing money. The rest of them constantly needed cash for movies and junk food and clothes. Dan and his dad needed money for rent and food. Abbi had seen his flat, and knew Dan's secret. His dad drank too much, and didn't seem to have a regular job. His mum had run off years ago.

Her own dad had gone to Australia when Abbi was ten, leaving her and her little brother Joe with their mother. But their mother worked hard selling houses and other property, and although they weren't rich there was always enough.

So when Dan said he wanted money, he meant it in a way that Abbi could only dream of. It was one of the interesting things about Stage School, she thought. People came from such different backgrounds, from all over the city. Matt's family owned a fruit and vegetable store in the Italian district, Jenna and her mum and sister lived near the university, where her mother worked at the library, she lived in a high-rise apartment block, Dan in an upstairs flat, and Lauren…Abbi shut her eyes and pictured again Lauren's big house, surrounded by lawns and trees. Lauren was so lucky.

Abbi's eyes snapped open. Maybe that was the answer to the mystery about Lauren! Maybe she was at home. She could pretend to leave for school, wait for her father to be at work, and then come back to that comfortable bedroom with its books and big windowseat. That's what I'd do, Abbi thought. We've probably been worrying for nothing.

"I'd love to audition again," she told Dan. "And this time, I promise not to get carried away."

☆CHAPTER FOURTEEN☆

A Cry for Help

Lauren woke up in an upstairs room in the hostel. The smell of stale smoke was in the pillow, the blankets, the air around her. It made her stomach roll dangerously.

She remembered coming back to the hostel, supported by Marco and Dragana, and struggling upstairs to this room. How long had she been sleeping?

She sat up and looked around the dim room. The green blind on the one small window was down. Lauren rolled it up and looked out. It was still daylight.

Dragana came into the room, and sat down on the bed. She leaned forward and looked at Lauren. "You had a dizzy spell," she said. "Too much work. If you give me your parents' number I call and they come and get you."

"I can get home by myself," said Lauren. She tried to get past Dragana's bulk and stand up.

Dragana pushed her gently, but firmly back. "I think you stay until your parents come," she said. "I don't want responsibility to let you go."

"I'm all right," Lauren insisted. This time, she managed to stand up. She noticed that her pockets were much lighter. Dragana must have taken all the squeegee money!

Marco was hovering anxiously at the bottom of the narrow staircase. "Angel Lauren," he said. "Are you well?"

Lauren wanted to ask him about the money, wanted to scream and shout at Dragana, but she had no energy. The important thing was to get out of the hostel, and home before her father missed her.

"I'm fine, Marco," she murmured. "I'll see you...soon."

The walk down the long hallway to the front door seemed to take forever. The kids were watching TV again in the darkened living room.

Once outside, Lauren took a deep breath of the autumn air, and felt better. She walked a block to the next bus stop, so she wouldn't have to wait in front of the hostel. It was frustrating how weak her legs felt.

The bus, once it came, stank of diesel. Lauren's stomach was still churning. They had gone a few stops when she knew she was going to be sick. She had to find a bathroom.

The glass wall of a downtown shopping mall gleamed ahead. Lauren got off the bus, ran through the automatic doors, and glanced up for the public toilet sign. Luckily, it was not too far, just down one level and to the right.

Lauren made it to the Ladies' room and was

desperately sick. Afterwards, she washed her face and collapsed against the tiled wall. Her watch said three thirty. She would never make it home on time.

What had happened to her? She had had a stomach virus before, but never such a violent one. Was there something wrong with the hot chocolate? the thought sprang into her mind suddenly. Had Dragana put something in her drink?

It seemed fantastic and right now she had no time to figure things out. She would have to invent an excuse for being late. Washing out her mouth one more time, she walked on wobbling legs to the bank of telephones just outside the Ladies' room. She dialled the Stage School number and pitched her voice down low.

"This is Abigail Reilly's mother. Could you page her for me? I have an important message for her."

The secretary on the other end put her on hold. Lauren slumped down on the bench by the phone, wanting to put her head between her knees to stop the faintness, but afraid to attract attention.

It seemed to be taking forever. Please let her be there, Lauren prayed. Then, suddenly, she heard Abbi's breathless voice.

"What's up, Mum?"

"It's not your mum," Lauren gulped. "It's me...Lauren." The sound of Abbi's voice made her want to cry. She looked up at the ceiling to keep the sob out of her voice.

"Lauren!" Abbi was whispering into the phone.

"Where are you?"

"It doesn't matter," Lauren said. "I'm going to call home and leave a message for Dad that I'm at your place, studying for a French test. If he phones, can you just back me up?"

"Sure, of course, but–"

"I've got to go. Thanks, Abbi."

"Wait a minute, don't hang up!" Abbi's voice was louder. "You sound awful. I'll only agree to this if you tell me where you are."

"I…can't," Lauren said.

"Then I'll have to tell your dad you haven't been at school and I don't know where you are. Come on, Lauren. Let me help you!"

"I'm at the Orchard Centre Mall," Lauren said in a low voice. "Abbi, please don't tell my dad."

"Stay there," Abbi demanded. "I'm coming to meet you. Just tell me where to find you."

"Bottom level, near Queen Street," Lauren gasped. There was no time to argue – she had to get back to the toilet.

"Don't move a muscle!" Abbi insisted. "It will take me half an hour to get there, but just wait."

Lauren banged down the phone and dashed for the Ladies' room again.

☆

Abbi hurried to the gym where the auditions were being held. She found Dan and Jenna, sitting on a bench on one side of the room, waiting for their turn to audition.

Dan was studying his face in a mirror. "If only my ears didn't stick out so far," he sighed. He ran his fingers through his spiky hair. "And my face is kind of lopsided – did you ever notice that?"

Abbi grabbed the mirror. "Forget your lopsided face, and your ears. I've found Lauren!"

"That's great!" Dan leaped to his feet. "Where is she?"

"She's all the way downtown, at the Orchard Centre Mall. I've got to go and meet her." Abbi's words tumbled out. "If her dad comes looking for her at Stage School, say we're at my place, studying together."

"But the auditions..." Dan began.

Jenna looked sympathetic. "I'm sure they would use you, with your beautiful skin...What's so important – is Lauren in trouble?"

Matt came rushing over. "The director is calling for...he wants us now!"

"Another time," Abbi looked longingly at the bank of lights, the wires and cameras.

"There is something wrong!" Jenna got to her feet. "Can't you tell us?"

"Break a leg, you three!" called Abbi as she left.

☆CHAPTER FIFTEEN☆

Abbi is Shocked!

Abbi rode impatiently down the escalator and scanned the almost empty mall for any sign of Lauren's fair head. Where was she?

And then Abbi saw a security guard in a navy uniform, escorting a small figure, bent almost double, out of the shopping centre.

"You can't hang around here," the woman was saying roughly. "Go and sleep off your drugs somewhere else."

For a second, Abbi was so surprised she couldn't move, or speak. This couldn't be Lauren. This girl looked like one of the homeless kids you saw on the street. Her hair was tousled under a bandanna, her clothes torn and dirty.

But it was Lauren's pale skin and grey eyes, looking much paler than usual. Abbi sprinted forward.

"Hey! That's my friend, leave her alone!"

To her shock, Lauren collapsed in Abbi's arms, smelling of smoke and sick, limp and exhausted.

"Well, if she's your friend, get her out of here," the security guard said. "We have too many girls like her using our facilities." She waited while Abbi put her arm around Lauren and helped her up the escalator.

Abbi was still struggling with the shock of seeing the usually neat, well-groomed Lauren looking like this.

"It's OK, just sit down here," she said, leading Lauren to a bench nearby. "How did you get in such a mess?"

"I don't know," Lauren was clutching her head. "It must be the flu – my head, and my stomach..."

"No, I mean, what are you doing down here at the mall, and why are you dressed like...like..."

"Like a squeegee kid?" There was a ghost of a smile on Lauren's pale lips. "Actually, I am a squeegee kid. I must have made loads of money before I got sick and Dragana took it all."

Lauren was delirious, Abbi thought. "Who's Dragana?"

Lauren groaned. "It's too long a story for now. What am I going to do?"

"Did you call your dad and say you were studying with me?" Abbi asked.

Lauren nodded. "I left a message."

"And I left a message on our machine that I didn't want to be disturbed, and wasn't taking calls. That should hold your dad until you get to my place and clean up. Then, if you still feel sick, you can call him to come and get you," Abbi said firmly.

"I have other clothes in my bag," Lauren mumbled.

"Great," Abbi nodded. "Come on, if you can walk." She took Lauren's bag and slung it over her shoulder with her own. Lauren looked too weak to carry a flea.

An hour later, staring into Abbi's bathroom mirror, Lauren looked almost like her old self – except for the colour of her face, which was still pasty grey.

"I can make it on the bus," she told Abbi. "I don't want Dad to worry."

"How's your mum?" Abbi asked.

Lauren's face in the mirror went another notch greyer.

"Sorry," Abbi said. "I shouldn't ask you questions now. Let's go. There's a bus due in five minutes."

As they went down the stairs in Abbi's apartment building, Lauren glanced gratefully at her friend. "I *will* tell you all about it," she promised. "You've been great."

"You can tell me on the bus," said Abbi. "I'm coming with you."

"You don't have to..."

"I want to make sure you get home. You still look terrible," Abbi insisted.

Lauren looked like she wanted to argue, but she clutched Abbi's arm while they waited for the bus, and leaned against her on the bus ride to her house.

"How's your stomach?" Abbi asked her friend.

Lauren made a face. "It's churning like a washing machine," she said, "and my head feels like somone's hitting it with a hammer. Let's talk about something else. What's been happening at Stage School?"

"Oh, you know, the usual," Abbi smiled. "Dan is trying to get a part in a television commercial for acne cream – Jenna and Matt are trying out, too."

Lauren bent her head so Abbi couldn't see her face. Better to get off the subject of Matt, Abbi thought. "I'm trying out, too, but I don't think I'm cut out for TV. Somebody videotaped my last audition, and I look like a hurricane on rollerblades. It was awful!"

Lauren tried to smile. The effect was pathetic. Abbi took Lauren's hand. "Listen. We know you haven't been going to Thorncrest this week."

Lauren turned an astonished face to Abbi's.

Abbi nodded. "I went to the school, and they said you hadn't registered. I don't blame you – the place looks as dry and dusty as old toast – just like my old school. But the point is, we're worried about you, Matt and Jenna and Dan and I. And we miss you. We want you back at Stage School. Things aren't the same without you."

Lauren looked away, out of the bus window. "Couldn't you talk to your father?" Abbi asked. "I mean, once your mum's feeling better, couldn't you at least talk to him about coming back? Tell him how much it means to you? It's got to be better than no school at all!"

Lauren shook her head. Stage School, Thorncrest – they both seemed so much less real than life on the street. Where you worked hard, and got dirty and hungry and sick, and where, if you had no friends, you might get shipped off to fight in some terrible war, like Marco! How could school compare with that?

At that moment, the bus rolled up to Lauren's stop and the brakes snorted.

"Thanks, Abbi," Lauren said, getting shakily to her feet.

"I'm going to make sure you don't fall off this bus," Abbi said, reaching out to steady her.

"It's all right," Lauren insisted, but Abbi was already standing by the door beside her, peering out at the street.

"Look, Lauren. Isn't that your dad?"

Mr Graham was pacing up and down the path in front of Lauren's house. If she'd been an artist, Abbi would have drawn him with smoke coming out of his ears when he saw the two of them together.

"Stay on the bus!" Lauren pleaded.

"Are you kidding? I'm not leaving you to face him all by yourself!"

Abbi's face was flushed. She was going to see this through to the end. They stepped off the bus right into the path of Lauren's furious father.

"Where have you been?" he demanded, taking Lauren by the shoulder. "And don't try to tell me you've been at school. I've had a call from them – you haven't been there all week!"

☆CHAPTER SIXTEEN☆

Back to the Hostel

"I think he would have killed me, if he could have," Abbi told her thunderstruck friends the next day in the Stage School canteen. "He blames everything that's happened to Lauren on us."

"What's he going to do?" Jenna's eyes were full of sympathy.

"Keep her locked away from us, that's for sure," Abbi sighed. "He's going to drive her to school every morning from now on, and pick her up at the end of the day. And she's not allowed any phone calls."

"Did she tell you what she was doing at the shopping mall?" Matt asked. He was working his way through his second morning doughnut. "Did you find out where she's been?"

"Not really," Abbi sighed again. "Only that she's been working as a squeegee kid, and making money."

"A squeegee kid?" Matt's eyebrows disappeared into his hair line.

"It doesn't make sense," Dan shook his head. "Our little Lauren, on the streets."

"And now she's a prisoner," Jenna said. "I wish there was a way to help her!"

"How did your audition go yesterday afternoon?" Abbi asked, changing the subject. She had her own ideas on how she was going to help Lauren!

"You should have seen us," Matt laughed. "We were a spotty crew! Then we washed our faces in Zit-Be-Gone, and presto, like magic, the beautiful clear complexions you see before you!" He ran his hand over Jenna's smooth cheek. A look flashed between them that both Dan and Abbi caught – as though they'd both received an electric shock.

"I'm sorry I missed it," Abbi said, sorrowfully. "It seems I'm not destined for TV."

"Don't be so sure," Dan laughed. "I'm working on a small surprise for you."

"Tell me!" Abbi jumped up from the canteen table, threatening to spill all their drinks.

"No, it wouldn't be a surprise if I did," Dan shook his head.

Just then, the bell rang for first period. Chaos erupted in the canteen as kids ran for the exits, carrying dance bags, instruments, backpacks and empty trays.

"See you at lunch," Abbi called to Jenna and Matt as they hurried off to the dance studio.

Five minutes later, the William S. Holly canteen was deserted, as empty as if five hundred kids had never been packed into it a moment before.

☆

Meanwhile, Lauren sat in an empty classroom at

Thorncrest, waiting for the other students to arrive. Her father had brought her to school at eight-thirty and had made sure she was registered and sitting at a desk before he left. If he could have chained me to this desk he would have, Lauren thought. She was sure if she got up and walked down the hall someone from the office would be watching and would pounce on her.

How could she possibly get away?

Lauren had been too sick and tired last night to think but this morning when she woke up, one thing had been crystal clear – Dragana must have put something in her drink at the restaurant. The chocolate would have masked the taste. She had never in her life had a stomach bug that came so fast and was so awful!

Dragana had wanted her out of the way, and it had worked. Maybe her plan had been to steal the money, and get Lauren in so much trouble with her parents that she would never come back to the hostel. Dragana had plans for Marco, Lauren was sure. She didn't want him to have money, friends, or any independence.

What was happening to Marco? Somehow, she had to get out of here and find out.

Her father had lectured her for an hour on how disappointed he was in her, how concerned for her mother, and how worried that Lauren was going completely off the rails. When he demanded to know where she had been, Lauren told him part of the truth.

"I've been volunteering, helping out at a shelter

for refugees," she said.

"I see." Her father paced up and down her bedroom floor. "That's very noble of you, but it's the lying that bothers me. Don't you see it wasn't right?"

"Yes, I see." Lauren was longing to be left alone, for this to stop. "I'm sorry."

Her father had finally left – vowing to treat her like a child if she insisted on acting like a child, and so here she was, waiting for the Thorncrest bell to ring, and the other girls to come pounding in, staring at her.

She had to get away.

☆

Her chance came at lunch time. The halls were crowded, just as at Stage School, only all the girls were wearing uniforms. Lauren had managed to squeeze into her old Thorncrest skirt and blazer. In her uniform, she knew it would be difficult to pick her out from the other girls.

Lauren eased her way towards the doors, keeping one eye on the office to make sure no one was watching.

Once outside, she made a run for it. Thorncrest was across the street from a large cemetery, and it was a short cut to the busy street beyond. Then round a few corners, down eight long blocks on McCann Street, and there she was!

The outside of the hostel beckoned innocently, but Lauren wasn't going to take a chance of getting stopped at the door by Dragana. She ducked down the narrow, weedy space between the hostel and the house next door, and squirmed through a hole in the fence into the back yard. She knew this was the route most of the kids used to the back door.

"Ooooh, Lauren, you look so nice!" one of the little girls from the hostel shrilled from the back porch.

Lauren held her finger up to her lips and smiled. The girl thought it was a game. She put her own finger up to her mouth and shook her head.

Lauren came close. "Where's Marco?" she whispered in the child's ear.

The little girl shook her head again. "Gone," she said softly.

"Gone?" Lauren stared at her. "Gone where?"

"They throwed him out because he stole some money, so Dragana said he couldn't sleep here no more."

"Do you know where he went?" Lauren whispered.

The little girl shook her head. "He cried!" she said. "He didn't say nothing. He just cried and went away, this morning."

Lauren straightened up. She tried once more to get some meaningful information out of the little girl. "Did the police take Marco away?"

This time, the child looked frightened. "No!" she said. "No policeman came. Marco just walked down the street." She pointed in the direction he had gone.

Lauren wondered briefly about confronting Dragana, and then thought better of it. Dragana would only lie. She wriggled back through the hole in the fence and started down McCann Street in the direction the little girl had pointed. She knew she should go back to Thorncrest. She couldn't even imagine what would happen when they discovered she wasn't in class, and phoned her father. She was sorry for causing all this trouble, but she had to look for Marco. She was his only friend in this whole huge city!

☆CHAPTER SEVENTEEN☆

Lauren Takes a Chance

"Where would I go, if I was Marco?" Lauren asked herself. The small girl had pointed downtown, in the direction of the squeegee kid corner where they had worked.

The gang of squeegee kids greeted Lauren like a long lost friend. "Madam, how elegant!" one of them teased, pointing to her school uniform. "Where did you get it, at the second-hand store?"

Lauren had forgotten she was wearing her uniform. "Have you seen Marco?" she asked. The kids were on the roadside, waiting for the lights to turn red. She only had a few seconds till they were gone.

"No, haven't seen him," they shook their heads. The light turned and, like a flock of hungry gulls, the kids darted into the still-moving traffic, their buckets and squeegees in their hands.

Lauren crossed at the lights and caught a bus going back in the direction of the university. Would Marco go back to the Friendship Centre? It was the only other place he knew where people had tried to help him.

But at the International Friendship Centre, Lauren got a shock.

"You've got some nerve, showing up here," Liz greeted her furiously. "It's kids like you that wreck everything for the others!"

"What are you talking about?" Lauren felt buffeted by her anger, but she stood her ground.

"That friend of yours – stealing money from our cash box – that's what I'm talking about!" Liz shook her finger at Lauren. "He watched me that day, taking the key out of the drawer and opening the box. All he had to do was waltz in here when I was out of the office and take it – and there was a great deal of money in it!"

"Marco!" Lauren gasped. "You think Marco robbed your cash box?"

"I think you were probably in it together. I'll tell you something. It's the last time I take a chance on somebody just because they look helpless!"

"I'm sure Marco didn't take your money," Lauren said firmly. She wondered how she had the courage to stand up to this angry, accusing woman. "I hope I get a chance to prove it to you, but right now, I have to find Marco."

☆

The trees in the park near the bus station threw short, noon day shadows when Lauren dodged across the busy street. People huddled on the benches – some with bags of food for the birds and squirrels. And there was Marco – on the bench where they had shared chocolate milk!

He was sitting with his head on his drawn-up

knees, his long hair hiding his face.

"Marco!" Lauren shouted.

But when the boy looked up, it wasn't Marco.

He looked sad, and lonely and hungry, but it was a different face and a different pair of eyes.

For a moment it seemed to Lauren, standing there in the flickering shadows of the trees, that the whole small square of park was full of homeless people – young and old, all cold and hungry – all needing help. She made a quick circuit of the park. Marco wasn't there.

There was one last place to look. Lauren waited for the lights at the intersection and ran across to the bus station.

She almost hoped Marco wouldn't be there, that he would have swallowed his pride and gone back to his cousin.

But as soon as she entered the waiting room she saw him, sitting on a bench as she had first seen him, looking anxiously around the room. It was the look of fear on his face that made her glad she had come, whatever might happen next.

"Lauren!" Marco stood up and swept the hair out of his eyes. "You are all right?"

"I'm fine," Lauren said. "I heard what happened."

"Nobody believe me," Marco looked down. "They all think I steal the money."

"Marco, did you tell Dragana about the cash box at the Friendship Centre?" Lauren asked.

Marco's eyes widened. "Yes, yes I did. She ask many questions when I first come about how I get money for taxi. She ask about key..." He shook his head angrily. "Oh, I am fool to tell her!"

"Marco, do you trust me?" Lauren asked, peering up into his face.

"With my life," Marco nodded soberly.

"Then I want you to come with me. I have some friends who will help you," Lauren said.

She paid for them both to get on the bus. On the ride back to Stage School, she described her friends. "Dan's an actor and Jenna's a dancer," she told him. "She's very smart and works incredibly hard. She and Matt won a prize trip to study dance in New York next spring."

"And who is Matt?" Marco asked.

Lauren could feel herself blush. "He's a dancer, too," she explained. "But he's not as serious as Jenna. He...he's strong and brave...you'll like him," she finished lamely.

"You like him, too!" Marco shook his head. "But I think he makes you sad."

"No...I mean, never mind that. Then there's Abbi," Lauren rushed ahead. "She's always dashing into things and getting crazy ideas, but sometimes her ideas are good, and she's a wonderful actress."

"But what will they think of me?" Marco asked. "It will be a big surprise, I think."

Lauren nodded. That was the understatement of the year. She hoped Jenna and Matt and Dan and Abbi would understand. "They'll look after you," she told Marco, hoping she believed it.

"But why do you go to another school, if these

are your friends you love so much?" Marco looked confused.

Lauren sighed. "It's complicated," she said. "I'll tell you about it some day. Right now, I want to know what happened after I left the hostel yesterday. Were you sick, too?"

"No," Marco shook his head. "I am fine. Dragana wants me to go with her to visit Ivan, the big guy with the hairy nose..."

Lauren nodded. That was the man she had seen fighting with Dragana the first day she came to the hostel. She had seen him hanging around the house several times since.

"I do not like Ivan," Marco said. "I tell Dragana I not work for him, and she is very, very angry. She goes out, and this morning she gets phone call asking where am I. She tells me to leave because police look for me, and I am thief."

Lauren grabbed his hand. "Don't worry. We'll sort it out. But I have to go back to my other school, and I may have trouble getting in touch with you for a while." She stood up. "Come on. We're here – this is William S. Holly."

☆CHAPTER EIGHTEEN☆

Stage School Takes Over

"I don't have time to explain the whole thing," Lauren shouted over the babble of voices in the canteen. "Please, just look after Marco for me until I get back at three thirty."

Jenna, Abbi and Matt stared at Lauren. She had appeared out of nowhere at the second lunch break, dragging this strange-looking tall boy after her.

Abbi was the first to recover. "Of course we will. His name is Marco? Don't worry. We'll look after him."

"And feed him," Lauren called over her shoulder as she dashed away. "He's hungry!"

Abbi smiled at Marco and he smiled nervously back.

"What are we supposed to do with him?" Matt asked. "And where did Lauren find him?"

"I am Marco Djuric," Marco said, with anxious dignity. "I am from Bosnia, a refugee. They think I steal money from the Centre place, but I do not. I am thrown out of my hostel, and perhaps authorities are looking for me."

"Sit down,' Abbi invited Marco. "You'll be fine here. Matt, give him some of your chips."

Matt passed some of his fries over to Marco who dived into them like a starving man.

"I'll go and get some sandwiches and stuff," Jenna said, uncoiling her long legs from the canteen table bench, and she hurried off in the direction of the food counter.

"We need a plan," Matt insisted. "If he's really in trouble, like he says, we can't just leave him here while we go off to classes."

"I don't think he's the only one in trouble," Abbi groaned. "Lauren will be killed if her father finds out she's left Thorncrest again! The school is bound to phone him."

"I'm glad she turned to us for help," Matt said. "I was really starting to wonder whether she still cared about us."

"Oh, she loves you all very much," Marco broke in. "Especially you, Matt. She thinks you are strong, and brave."

Matt seemed to swell. "We're all Lauren's friends here," he motioned around the table.

Abbi sighed. Poor Lauren. Matt never seemed to understand that it was not his friendship she wanted.

"I've got a first period spare," Matt went on. "Marco can hang out with me till we figure out what to do."

"Here's some lunch," Jenna made her way back through the crowded tables with a tray of coke, sandwiches and a large slice of pie.

Marco looked like he might faint with joy. "Lauren is right," he sighed. "You are being the best!"

As they left the canteen, Dan came dashing up. "Guess what? Matt and I, and Jenna got call-backs for the zit cream commercial. Three thirty sharp, in the auditorium."

He stopped short at the sight of Marco. "Hello."

"This is Lauren's friend, Marco," Abbi introduced them. "Marco, this is Dan."

Marco gave a bow. "I am happy to meet all friends of Lauren."

"What are we going to do if Lauren's not back at three thirty?" Jenna whispered to Abbi as they followed the boys down the hall.

"She will be," Abbi said.

☆

Lauren willed the bus to go faster. It seemed to hit every red light on the way downtown. She had messed up everything! Marco would never be in this trouble if she hadn't taken him to the Friendship Centre and the hostel in the first place. Now he was not only a refugee, but a fugitive!

And who knows, she told herself, Dragana might have been nicer to him if I hadn't interfered. I just stuck my nose into something I didn't understand at all!

On top of that, Lauren thought, I should never, never have agreed to leave Stage School. That's my school, those are my friends. How could I let my parents persuade me to leave? Lauren pounded her fist into the backpack on her lap.

Now there was construction work slowing them – the traffic was down to one lane. I could walk faster than this bus, Lauren thought, chewing her nails. Finally, three blocks from the corner where the squeegee kids worked, she got off and ran.

"Can anyone spare me a squeegee and bucket?" Lauren begged as she ran up to the squeegee kids at the familiar corner.

"Sorry," one of the guys shook his head. "No such thing as a spare."

"Ask at the garage," another suggested. "Look out, light's red."

Lauren left them swinging into action with their pails of soapy water and ran to the corner garage. More waiting! All the attendants were busy.

"I can't lend you a squeegee," a tall, blond car mechanic laughed, when he had a second to talk to Lauren. "No way! We lose half a dozen a day to that bunch of vultures!" he motioned to the squeegee kids.

"I can pay," Lauren fumbled in her bag. She had some money in there somewhere.

"Try the shop across the street," the man said. "They keep a stock for the honest squeegee kids."

There was no time for trips to the store! Lauren ran back to the corner. "Here," she held out her cash to a tall squeegee kid, nicknamed The Loafer. "Rent your squeegee equipment to me for an hour. Take a break."

The Loafer looked confused, then laughed. "It's a deal," he said. "I get my squeegee back in an hour, right?"

"Thanks, Loafer," Lauren said breathlessly. "You'll get it back." The light was turning. She grabbed the pail of soapy water, sloshing some of it on her skirt, and dived into the lines of slowly moving cars.

Somehow, she remembered to smile. Drivers smiled back, and nodded yes. Lauren cleaned windows as she had never cleaned before. Up, down, swoosh sideways, on to the next.

In an hour she had cleaned fifty of them, and earned almost enough to pay the Friendship Centre back and clear Marco's name. Just a few more cars...

She could do one more, before the lights changed. She leaned into the next car window as it moved forwards slowly. The man behind the wheel was already shaking his head, no, angrily.

Lauren straightened up, the squeegee frozen in her hand, dripping on to a familiar blue car.

The stunned face of her father stared up at her. "Lauren!"

"Dad! What are you doing here!" The shock of seeing him sent Lauren reeling backwards, almost into the path of a van. The van blew its horn and the driver shouted curses out of the window.

Lauren's father slammed on his brakes. The car behind almost ran into him. Angry horns blew on both sides.

"Dad! The light's green. You have to move the car!" Lauren shouted

"Get in!"

"I can't!"

"I'm not moving this car until you get in!" he yelled at her.

Someone was going to get hurt. Lauren ran round the front of the car and pulled open the door on the passenger side.

"Get that filthy bucket out of my car," her father hissed between clenched teeth, as she climbed into the front seat with her squeegee and bucket of soapy water.

"No," Lauren said. "It belongs to one of the other kids. I'm just renting it..."

Her father's face was white with anger. The car surged forward through the intersection, turned right at the next corner and stopped. His hands were gripping the wheel so hard his knuckles were purple. Most of the water sloshed out on to the car's carpet.

"Look what you've done! What's your mother going to think?"

Lauren opened the door.

"Where do you think you're going?"

"To take the bucket and squeegee back. They're not mine," Lauren said.

"You...my daughter, you're one of these..."

"Squeegee kids? Yes, I am, at least for a while. I'll be right back, Dad."

Lauren got out of the car and strode back to the corner. The other kids threw her curious looks as the traffic swept by.

"You OK? You know that guy?" one of the older girls asked.

"I'm OK," Lauren said. "He's my dad. Listen, I

have to go. Can you make sure this bucket and squeegee get back to The Loafer? I borrowed them from him."

"Sure," the girl nodded. "Leave them by that telephone pole. I'll keep an eye on them – no problem."

Her father was still gripping the steering wheel when she got back to the car. Showdown time, Lauren thought.

She took a deep breath. This time she was not going to let her dad get his own way, or stop her from saying what he didn't want to hear.

But he began to shout as soon as she was in the car. "I was on my way to pick up your mother," he started. "They've released her from the hospital on a trial basis. Everything at home should be as perfect and quiet as we can make it. I was going to pick you up at school – we were all going to go home together, and now I find you here!"

"I know, Dad, but I had to make some money..."

"If you needed money, all you had to do is ask. You know that. You don't have to be out here like some street kid."

"It's more complicated than that," Lauren said. "I need your help, but I couldn't talk to you about it when you had Mum to worry about...shouldn't you go and get her?"

"We will both go and get your mother. And while we're on the way, you'll explain to me what you're doing here." He pounded the steering wheel.

"No, wait. I can't go with you. There's something I have to do…" Lauren put her hand on her father's arm. "I have to…go back to Stage School."

"Lauren, whatever trouble you're in will have to wait." Her father's lips were set in a grim line. "I'm counting on you to come with me now, and pick your mother up from the hospital."

Lauren thought of her mother, waiting anxiously at the hospital. She thought of Marco and the others, waiting at William S. Holly for her to return. Meanwhile, her father was starting the car. What was she going to do?

☆CHAPTER NINETEEN☆

Where is Lauren?

"It's twenty past three." Abbi was pacing up and down the hall in front of the Stage School auditorium. "Where is Lauren? It's my night to baby-sit my brother Joe, after school. I can't wait around, and you three all have call-backs for the acne cream commercial – you lucky things!"

"I'm sorry you missed the first audition," Jenna said. "You would have had a call-back for sure."

"That's OK." Abbi shrugged. "But what are we going to do about Marco?"

Matt, Jenna and Dan were all waiting to be called inside the auditorium for their second audition. "Couldn't you take Marco home with you?" Matt asked. Marco was standing awkwardly, a little way away from them. They'd been hauling him to their classes all afternoon. By now, he looked thoroughly dazed.

"Are you serious? My mother has a fit if she comes home and finds one of you guys there," Abbi reminded Matt. "Just imagine if she finds a strange seventeen-year-old guy in our apartment. She'll go straight through the ceiling!"

A production assistant poked her nose out through the auditorium doors. "We're ready for the next bunch," she said. She was a short, slim girl with glasses and a clipboard.

"That's us," said Dan. "We'll have to take Marco into the audition, too."

"Just be quiet, Marco," Matt warned him. "Don't say anything, and we'll be fine. There'll be so many people, they won't notice one more."

But they did notice. The sharp-eyed production assistant looked up from her clipboard. "Who's this?" she asked, eyeing Marco.

"He's Marco," Jenna said quickly. "He's visiting us from the former Yugoslavia."

"He's just observing our training," Dan added. "He's very quiet – just watches, doesn't say anything."

Marco tossed back his hair and tried to grin. The production assistant was staring at him in a very peculiar way.

"Do that again..." she said.

Marco shrugged and looked at the others for help.

"You...the tall one. Throw your hair back again. Say something."

"He doesn't speak English very well..." Jenna hurried to explain.

"That's perfect. Say, 'Hello, Grandma. It's so good to hear your voice.'" The assistant was still looking at Marco as if he were a prize pup in a dog show.

Marco looked horribly embarrassed.

"Go ahead," Dan whispered. "Say it."

Haltingly, Marco said the line. "Hel–lo, Grandma. It's so good to hear your voice."

The assistant clasped her hands together in joy. "Wait here. Whatever you do, don't go away. I'll be right back."

Matt, Jenna and Dan exchanged astonished glances.

"I don't have grandma," Marco said.

"It's OK," Matt told Marco, "this is show business."

The production assistant came hurrying back with the producer, a short plump man with a permanent worried frown.

"Is this the kid?" he said. "Let's hear him!"

Marco said his line again. The wrinkles on the producer's brow vanished. "Amazing!" he breathed. "We interview five hundred kids with fake accents and this boy turns up by accident! Are you an actor? Who's your agent?"

"He's a student," Jenna broke in. "Just visiting. He doesn't have an agent."

"You mean, he's the real thing?" the producer was hugging himself with joy. "Come this way, come this way." They were leading Marco away.

"Wait a second," Jenna said. "What are you talking about, here?" Jenna could look very adult and formidable when she wanted. The producer stopped.

"We're talking TV commercials, billboards, newspaper and bus stop ads. We're talking big money, baby."

Jenna's eyes shot sparks. Nobody called her baby.

Dan got between them. "What about our acne cream call-backs?" he asked.

"Oh, sure," the producer waved a careless hand. "Over there." He pointed in the direction of some lights and cameras. "Of course, we'll have to test him, and show him to the account executives, but can't you just see this kid? He'll be wonderful: 'Hello, Grandma, is that you?'" The producer imitated Marco's accent. "Who says this isn't a wonderful business?"

Jenna motioned to Matt and Dan. "You two go ahead. I'd better stick with Marco and make sure he doesn't get into trouble," she whispered.

☆

Lauren glanced at the hospital clock as they walked into the front entrance. Three forty five. She gulped back her feelings and stared straight ahead as she stood beside her father in the elevator.

Her mother was smiling as they came into her room. She was sitting in an armchair in her ordinary clothes, and she looked much better.

Lauren took a deep breath. "Hi, Mum," she said. "Can we talk, just the two of us, before we go home?"

"Lauren!" Her father's voice behind her was harsh and full of warning. "Not now!"

"I need to talk to Mum," Lauren said. On the way here, in the car, she had decided that her mother must not come home to a house full of anger and silence. If she could, she was going to tell her everything – now, before they left the hospital.

"I think that's a good idea," her mother said. She looked over Lauren's shoulder at her husband. "Why don't you get some tea, dear."

Lauren heard her father make a strangled noise in his throat. Then the door shut and his footsteps echoed away down the hall.

"I've been doing a lot of thinking," her mother smiled. "But you go first."

Lauren sat on the carefully made bed and took her mother's hand. Where should she start? Marco, she thought. I'll tell her about Marco.

Her mother's eyes were huge when she'd finished her story. "You were out there…on the street…" she began.

"There are lots of kids out there. And I want to help. And Mum, I can't go back to Thorncrest," Lauren rushed on. "I don't belong there. I'm not sure what I want to do, but I know it has to be something at William S. Holly."

Her mother's eyes filled with tears. "You seem so grown up…talking this way."

"That's another thing," Lauren stroked her mother's hand. "I want to talk to you, tell you how I feel and about my friends. I don't want to pretend any more. Sorry, Mum, but I'm never going to be that good little girl in the stiff frilly dress that you wanted me to be."

Her mother sighed. "It will be good to talk. I want to try to understand who you are…what you want to be. It seems like we've both learned a lot in the last few days. We'll talk to your father."

☆CHAPTER TWENTY☆

A Brilliant Future

"The cash from that commercial is going to come in handy." Dan was walking on air next Monday morning when the gang met in the William S. Holly canteen.

"How much do you think it will pay?" Jenna asked. She was looking forward to having spending money in New York.

"We haven't seen the contracts yet," said Matt. He was gobbling his second sticky bun of the morning. "It depends on how often they show the commercial, and where. But it should be at least a hundred and fifty."

"And it's more, if you have lines to say," Abbi chimed in, "like Marco does."

"Hello, Grandma, how are you?" they all chorused. The story of Marco's lucky break had spread throughout the school. His commercial would be shot this week, and in the meantime he was staying with Matt's family and helping out in the store.

"You should see that guy work," Matt said, "and he eats even more than I do."

Just then, Lauren and Abbi came up to the table. "We've talked to the lawyer your sister found," Lauren told Jenna. "He says Marco has an excellent chance for refugee status."

"Especially now that he's a star," Dan laughed.

"Speaking of Marco," said Lauren, "I have an announcement to make." She turned to Matt. "Can you get me on the school PA system again?"

"S-sure," he stammered. "But let me get this straight. You want to make an announcment to the whole school?"

Lauren shoved her fair hair behind her ears. "I want everyone to hear it," she nodded firmly. "Let's go – before classes start."

A few minutes later, Lauren's friends were stunned to hear her clear, musical voice coming over the school's public address system.

"Hi! This is Lauren Graham. I'd like to announce a special meeting for anyone interested in helping homeless kids this winter. It's getting cold out there and they need coats, boots, anything we can spare. If you'd like to help me organize a group to help the homeless kids in our city, meet in Room 263 after school."

"Wow!" Abbi clapped her hands. "Listen to Lauren. She sounds like a different person."

"She sounds like her real self," Jenna grinned.

"And it's a great idea to collect warm clothes for kids on the street," Dan added. "I'd like to be part of that!"

A few minutes later, Lauren and Matt were back. Lauren strode across the canteen, her head up and her face glowing. Matt followed her proudly.

"Did you hear that?" he crowed. "What a pro!"

"We all heard, and we'll all help on your committee," Jenna promised.

"You've already helped me so much," Lauren smiled. "The lawyer, and the refugee organization you found for Marco…"

"That's my super-organized sister," Jenna shrugged. "She knows a million people."

"What's going to happen to Dragana?" asked Dan. "Are they going to close the hostel?"

Lauren shook her head. "I don't know. The police are investigating a whole ring that preys on helpless refugees, finding them illegal jobs and then taking their money. They think Dragana was part of that. I had to make a statement to the police about everything I'd seen and heard at the hostel. And they're looking into the theft at the Friendship Centre. They don't believe Marco did it any more."

"Of course he didn't!" Abbi sounded indignant. "Poor Marco, falling into the hands of that woman. You two were lucky to escape alive!"

"I was lucky you came to rescue me at the mall," Lauren said. "That's when I realized how much better off I was compared to the other street kids. I had a friend like you to come and help. I'm just sorry you missed your TV audition!"

"Hey! No need to be sorry," Dan jumped up. "I haven't had a chance to show Abbi my surprise. All of you meet me in the video room in ten minutes."

Ten minutes later they were sprawled on comfortable chairs, pulled up in front of a TV monitor. Dan hit the video play button.

The image of Abbi, wearing rollerblades, skated towards the camera, bottle in hand. Then there was a quick, brilliant collage of shots of her falling. The contents of the bottle flew in all directions, until even the camera lens was washed in orange fizzy drink.

The five of them were rolling with laughter by the end.

"Like that?" Dan asked with a sideways grin. "So did the advertising agency. They're thinking about using it. So you might get to be a star after all, Abbi."

Abbi wiped tears of laughter from her eyes. "I looked like an idiot," she gasped, "but it's a great commercial! I love the way you've put it together."

Dan basked in Abbi's praise. "Maybe someday you'll recognize my other talents," he said.

"You're all so talented," Lauren's eyes danced from one to the other. "I'm so happy for Marco, and the rest of you, but I'm a bit jealous."

"You want to act in a TV commercial?" Matt looked surprised. "What about your stage fright?"

"I'm getting over it," Lauren smiled. She looked around the faces of her four friends. This was where she belonged, after all, and she would prove it. "I'm going to try not to be afraid of anything, from now on."

Preview the next

STAGE SCHOOL

NOW...

Dan – Clowning Around

☆CHAPTER ONE☆

The Bag Man

"Hey, give it back." Dan made a lunge for the large brown paper bag.

His best friend Matt pulled it away, slamming his shoulder against a locker in the process. "What's in it? Must be something really good."

"My lunch," Dan mumbled, hoping Matt would let the subject drop.

"Lunch?" Matt laughed and uncurled the top of the bag. "What do you have? A tape worm or something?"

"I get hungry," Dan answered, wishing he'd kept the bag hidden. He shook his head. How could he explain to Matt? He would never understand the way Dan and his father lived.

"A loaf of bread?" Matt looked puzzled. "Not even whole wheat. You've gotta put better stuff in that scrawny body of yours. Matt poked at one of Dan's arms.

Easy for Matt to say. With his parents owning a

grocery store, he always had a supply of good food. Dan suspected Matt would have been a girl magnet regardless of what he put in his athletic dancer's body. What could Dan tell him? Nothing. So he changed the subject. "Did you see the Bond movie on TV last night?"

"There was a Bond movie?" Matt was about to hand back the bag, but snatched it away again. "And you didn't phone me?" he said, laughing.

Once more Dan blushed. He raised one eyebrow Bond style. "Don't you know our phone lines are tapped? The whole Western security system would have been compromised." Dan reached out his hand. He looked down the hall, in cool James Bond style and suddenly panicked. Abbi was coming. He felt his face burning as he snatched back his lunch, pitched it in the top of his locker and banged the door shut.

He glanced back at Abbi. Good, she hadn't noticed.

Bounding down the hall, Abbi Reilly's blue eyes sparkled and her gold-blonde curls bounced. She looked ready to burst with good news. Which was strange, Dan thought, considering she had a test in her worst subject this morning. He wished he could have called her last night to remind her.

Always the clown, what can Dan do when his troubles are no laughing matter? And will Abbi ever take him seriously? Read on in...

Stage School 5

☆Dan – Clowning Around☆

Have you read the other Stage School stories?

Abbi - Make or Break

Abbi - Blind Ambition

Jenna - Dancing Dreams

Lauren - Drastic Decisions

Dan - Clowning Around

Matt - Heartbreak Hero